Edge

Killers Inc. #2

Charity Parkerson

Punk & Sissy Publications

Copyright

—Warning: This book is intended for readers over the age of 18. Some of my books contain allusions to past abuse and trauma.

Editor: BZ Hercules & Consultants

Cover art: Charity Parkerson

Contents

About the Author

Author Note

THIS SERIES IS ABOUT trained assassins. Assassins aren't born. They're forged. So, this series deals with several elements that shape hired killers. It has darker elements such as abuse, murder, and abduction.

Introduction

AFTER A SHORT ABDUCTION, Mickey finds himself at the center of his kidnapper's obsession. He's not mad about it.

No one has ever accused Edge of being sane. He was raised to be a killer, and that's what he is. But nothing matters to Edge like his found family, and Edge thought Mickey planned to hurt one of his, so he snatched him. It wasn't a long, drawn-out dilemma. He discovered pretty quickly he was wrong. However, Mickey's cool-under-pressure attitude has him intrigued. Plus, he's always had a thing for green eyes. He's fascinated.

Mickey isn't one to kick up a fuss. So Edge took him for a little ride. He apologized. It's all good. Except the guy is kind of hot and Mickey isn't immune. With Mickey's high-power boss making deals with Edge's family, they're always in each other's sphere. What could tasting him hurt? Apparently, a lot, especially him.

Edge is the second book in Charity Parkerson's Killers Inc. series where hired assassins and their ilk find the love that finally saves them. These are best enjoyed when read in order.

Chapter One

THE WAY HENRY'S FACE lit as he joked with Beau always fascinated Mickey. The salt in his pepper beard caught the light as he threw his head back and roared with laughter. Mickey found the entire scene riveting. No one acted this way with Beau. Beau Bosi was the biggest weapons dealer on the west coast. He was deadly and could be extremely cruel. Yet there was this whole other side to him at home. Just like Beau, Henry was also two different people. One was the guy who ruthlessly protected everyone under Beau's roof and killed without guilt or mercy. Then there was this guy who cut up with Beau like they were both high school pranksters. Sometimes, Mickey wondered if there was something wrong with him for the way that made him feel.

"You're in love with him."

Mickey blinked. His gaze jerked to Kylo. Kylo was Beau's adorable husband, who was as sweet as they came. He was a Little and a breath of fresh air. Mickey worked as his personal guard. Watching Henry and Beau had given him something to do while Kylo painted him.

"What?"

Kylo nodded toward where Henry still teased Beau. "Henry. You love him."

A bright smile exploded across Mickey's face. "What did I do to make you think that, and how can I make it stop?"

Kylo shrugged. His baby blue eyes stayed locked on the canvas. "It's in your eyes when you look at him."

"It most certainly is not."

Kylo's gaze moved to hold his stare. "It's okay. I think we've all hopelessly loved at least one person."

Mickey huffed. He adored Kylo, but Kylo was a romantic. Mickey realized that actually made him easier to talk to, but fuck. "Life would be easier if I was in love with him, but I'm not. He's more like a dad to me."

Kylo's eyes twinkled with mischief. "Sometimes a daddy is so much hotter."

Mickey snorted. "No, thank you. I'm not interested in being spanked. Sometimes, their relationship mesmerizes me." He nodded toward where Beau and Henry laughed together. "I don't think either of them is like that with anyone else. Maybe it makes me lonely, I don't know, but I'm definitely not in love with him."

Kylo glanced behind him. He shrugged. "Henry has been with Beau more years than he hasn't. Of course they're close." He smiled. "Just think, one day, we'll be just like them."

Mickey snorted again. "Are you kidding? We're already like that."

They exchanged a look and burst into laughter. Kylo was definitely every bit as much his friend as his responsibility. He had no reason to be lonely. Kylo was right. They had each other. His humor disappeared as a familiar face strolled into the room. Edge Agafonov was a Russian-born assassin. A sniper—one known for his ability to hit any target from any height. He was brown-haired and brown-eyed, which sounded unremarkable but was anything but. His eyes had a bit of gold to them, and he was just sex on two legs, and no, Mickey didn't know how to explain that. He just had a sultry walk, voice, and stare. The guy would make one hell of an actor for any part where he had to seduce someone. If they had run into each other on the street, Mickey would be obsessed. He would chase the guy so hard, Edge would be forced to kill him. Unfortunately, that was not how they had met.

Out of the blue, several months back, Edge had held a gun to his head and forced him into a van. They'd gone on a short ride to an even shorter interrogation session. Henry had shown up and made it clear to the Agafonov boys that Beau wasn't a man to be fucked with and his people were off limits. Don't get him wrong, Mickey hadn't been worried or hurt. He had known Henry waited in a nearby car, and followed. There hadn't been a second where he felt in danger, but still. The move had not endeared Edge to him. Oddly, though, Edge acted like that day made them besties and it confused the fuck out of Mickey.

Beau appeared behind Kylo. He set his hands on Kylo's shoulders and eyed the painting. "It's looking amazing, baby." He bent and kissed Kylo's neck.

The instant hot lust that etched Kylo's features had Mickey turning his head.

Unfortunately, that left him staring into slightly golden eyes. That wasn't a better choice. He couldn't look away.

"We should take a nap. The boys are going for a ride."

"Okay, Daddy." Kylo stood. "Thank you for sitting with me."

A smile tugged at Mickey's lips at Kylo's words. He always acted like Mickey wasn't an employee doing his job. It was nice. Kylo made the place feel like a home—like this was a family. Like Mickey had a choice. He would choose Kylo, but it was still his job.

"Of course. I had fun. Enjoy your nap."

Beau winked as he walked away, with Kylo in tow.

Mickey shook his head. Everything had changed since Beau met Kylo. He prayed that never changed. Unfortunately, Kylo and Beau's departure left Mickey with nothing to do but focus on their visitor. Still, he let Henry take the lead.

"We have a warehouse to check."

Mickey nodded and held his silence. Outside of Kylo, he never talked much. He didn't have anything to say.

Edge watched him with so much intensity, it was almost uncomfortable. He couldn't look directly at the guy.

"Hello, Mickey."

Chill bumps rose on Mickey's skin. Heat, humor, and condescension coated each heavily accented word. It didn't even make sense the way his voice affected him, and Mickey wanted to feel it against his skin. The fucking bastard.

Mickey gave him his most bored-looking nod while keeping his face blank. "Edge." There. Now they could just not speak.

They headed for the garage.

Edge was so close to his heels that Mickey had never been more self-conscious. "How are you today?"

Laughter dripped from every word. Edge knew he made Mickey uncomfortable, and it pissed him off. Mickey chose to flip the switch. He pasted on an overly bright smile. "I'm awesome, actually. No one kidnapped me, so overall a top-notch morning. How about you? Did you squeeze in an abduction before breakfast?"

Edge rolled his eyes. Even that was hot. "Don't be absurd. Kidnapping isn't my usual style. I shot someone between the eyes about two this morning, though. Do you count that as before breakfast or the middle of the night?"

At some point, Mickey forgot he was only toying with Edge. "It depends. Did you go to sleep afterward?"

"Just a quick two hours."

"Middle of the night," Mickey said, finding his answer.

"Then, no. I was a good boy before breakfast."

Mickey practically felt Henry roll his eyes. He thought all the Agafonov boys were just that—boys. Henry didn't want the responsibility of them and didn't understand why Beau brought them in for their upcoming drop. They had always kept Beau safe without ex-

tra help. Henry was a little bitter over
it. They would do as told, though. Following orders kept everyone alive and
paid. Mickey just wished he didn't feel
Edge's stare from the back seat. That
was the only thing making him think
he couldn't do this.

If Edge made Mickey uncomfortable
with his constant stare, he didn't show
it. It was rare for Edge not to have
someone's number at first glance. He
couldn't read Mickey. Every time he
thought Mickey might show some real
emotion, he turned all fake smiles and
joking. The way his eyes swam with

laughter at Edge's expense always fascinated Edge because that faked humor hid a killer. The guy was deadly. He was the perfect personal guard for Kylo. In fact, Edge was surprised Beau had sent Mickey with them today. Mickey likely didn't leave Kylo's side often. In fact, Edge was shocked by this entire outing.

Beau Bosi wasn't a man who needed help. He employed his own army. But apparently, one of their longtime clients asked to meet at a different location for their next drop. Something about the situation had Beau's senses tingling. He wanted people his client wouldn't recognize working reconnaissance on the building. By drop time, his brother, Tracker, would have every inch of the place wired for sound and video while the team stayed in position to massacre the entire lot of them if they pulled any bullshit. It was a fairly easy assignment for Edge's people. Usually, they were up against people as trained as they were. That made it a little harder to get the upper hand other than having the element of perfectly planned surprise. This was nothing. Still, it was best to do a walk-through before they got started tonight. He didn't want any mistakes.

The building was located deep inside the warehouse district in Tecate. It was insane how easily Henry and Mickey crossed the border. No one even looked their way. At first glimpse of anything Bosi-related, everyone turned their head. Edge wondered what it must be like to wield so much power. It was equally crazy how everyone already knew Edge's family by association and also didn't question their actions.

The district where the meeting was being held had dried up decades ago, leaving empty buildings filled with nothing but old equipment, dust, and rats. Edge understood why Beau was reluctant to trust this new venue. His client claimed heat was on him at their usual spot near the ports, but a two-hour drive one way to a new location left for a lot of room for shit to go wrong.

Edge spotted his team's van parked a few streets over before they reached their destination. Tracker would be inside the vehicle, readying his surveillance. When they reached the warehouse, Henry cautiously stepped from the vehicle. Mickey waited for a few beats before following, as if they always worked together the same way. They did a quick tour of the building before regrouping outside. He didn't see a single member of his team, but he knew they were there.

"Henry, you'll be with Beau, correct?"

Henry dipped his chin. "They'll immediately become suspicious if I'm not at his side."

Edge nodded. He glanced Mickey's way, trying his damnedest to not get distracted by gorgeous green eyes. Between his eyes and his blond hair, he was the sexiest creature Edge had ever seen.

"How are you with heights?"

Mickey shrugged. "Pretty unbothered."

"Good. You'll come with me." He headed for the side of the building without looking to see if he was obeyed. Edge was the team leader. People didn't question him.

Like the good soldier, Mickey was right on his heels when Edge turned. "How are you with scaling buildings?"

A wicked light flashed in Mickey's eyes. "I grew up homeless. The roofs of businesses were the perfect place to get some sleep without worrying about getting attacked."

Damn. Every time he opened his mouth, Edge liked him more. "Good. Let's go. I want to make sure you can actually get up, down, and out of dodge if shit goes sideways."

Mickey shrugged and headed to a nearby fire escape. He had to jump to grab the bottom rung, but he got it on the first try. Mickey tested its strength before swinging himself upward. In no time, he disappeared on the rooftop. His head peeked over the edge. He was smiling. Edge didn't bother with the ladder. He easily scrambled up the side of the building. Getting high for the best shots was his thing.

"Impressive."

Edge flashed Mickey a smile at the compliment. "Well, if you spend over a decade of your life being tortured into compliance, you'll move your ass up a wall." Edge moved to where his gear waited for him without looking to see Mickey's reaction. He didn't need anyone's pity. His spine was steel, and he was richer than he could have ever dreamed possible because of what he had suffered. Life moved on.

He unzipped his bag. "We still have a long while before Henry gets back with Beau and the shipment. Put this in." Edge handed Mickey an earpiece. "You'll hear everything I do. How's everything coming together, Tracker?"

Mickey put the earpiece in his ear while Edge scanned the area. He spotted Ridge on a rooftop next door. Field and Shore would be hidden inside nearby buildings, setting up for ground fire.

"Good. Scout is still out canvassing the area. Beau was right to find this odd. Everything about this gig has my neck hairs crawling. This dude best not get us killed, or worse, locked up."

Edge flashed Mickey a tight smile. "Yeah. Guess I should've mentioned I have Mickey here."

"My statement stands, but hey, Mickey."

"Hey."

Edge fought a laugh at Mickey's awkward-sounding hey. It was obvious the guy wasn't much of a conversationalist.

"Hey, Mickey. Is that fine-ass zaddy with you?"

Mickey shook his head as Field's voice cut through their conversation. "He's headed back to get Beau."

"Ah, man. I missed him. Just wait. He shall be mine. MWHAHA."

Edge snorted at Field's obnoxious evil laugh. He dug deeper into his bag and pulled out his rifle and got set up. Then he pulled a smaller gun out for Mickey. "Take this."

Mickey waved away the offer. "I'm good." He pulled two weapons out that were hidden beneath his shirt. Mickey put them away. "If all else fails." He whipped out a scary-looking knife.

Edge gave him a sharp nod. "Good. I don't think anything will go down tonight, but you never know."

"Um, guys. There's an issue. We have another team rolling in."

Edge went on alert. He had his eye to his scope in an instant, scanning the area at Scout's claim. "Fuck! Everyone not already at least three buildings away, move your ass now. Tracker, pick us up four clicks to the east and call Beau. He was right. It's the goddamn Mexican Army. This was a setup." He turned to tell Mickey to head out, but Mickey was already climbing over the edge, heading in the right direction. Edge quickly broke down his weapon, gathered his gear, and was on his heels. When he reached Mickey, cutting through the warehouse next door, he had his phone to his ear already filling in his people. Mickey spoke quickly, but he wasn't even out of breath as he jogged the just over two miles to where Tracker waited. They all reached the van at the same time. Tracker was already pulling away as they jumped inside. Rain and Shadow had been with Tracker, waiting until they were needed, which was absolute worst-case scenario in this instance. With the entire crew loaded, they quietly left the scene behind.

Edge didn't breathe properly until they were back on American soil. "Welp. This is why we're always at the site hours before anyone else would be."

"Thank fucking God," Ridge muttered. They were all rightfully irritated. It had been years since they had a job go badly.

"This wasn't a failure." Everyone looked Mickey's way at the pragmatic-sounding statement. He shrugged. "Beau said something wasn't right. You proved he knew what he was talking about. With your help, no one got killed or arrested. It was a good day. Of course, it won't be for the client who betrayed Beau, but that's not our problem."

Mickey was right.

Edge watched as shoulders relaxed and team members started chatting amongst themselves. He was amazing. "Thank you for that." Edge silently mouthed the words for only Mickey. The last thing he needed was for his team to get shaken in any way.

When they got to Beau's, Henry waited outside, looking ready to explode. As soon as Mickey stepped out of the van, Henry was on him. He patted Mickey as if looking for injuries.

Mickey made a soothing motion. "I'm okay. No one got anywhere near me." He motioned over his shoulder. "These guys are amazing. They had us out of there before anything happened."

Henry nodded. The relief written on his face had Edge enthralled and disappointed. It was obvious Henry loved Mickey. Even if Mickey didn't return his feelings, Henry would probably kill anyone Mickey touched. That had a million other questions brewing inside him.

"Would you like to check me for injuries too, Daddy?" Field skipped Henry's way, being obnoxious in a way only he could accomplish. The giant red-haired joke-ster loved being the center of attention.

Henry sighed like Field made him tired in a single sentence. But his attention stayed with Mickey. "Kylo doesn't know anything happened today. Let's keep it that way."

Mickey nodded, looking serious. "Of course."

Henry gave him a sharp nod.

Field slid in behind him. He squeezed Henry's shoulders. "Maybe I should check you instead."

Henry pinched the spot between his eyes.

Field slipped a sucker into Henry's pock-et. "For later. You can suck it and think of me."

Edge watched the entire exchange with growing horror. There was a very real chance Field would get killed.

Mickey dipped his chin, motioning toward the garage. "May I speak with you in private for a moment?"

Edge tried to hide his surprise. Mickey never purposely had anything to do with Edge. Edge didn't hesitate to join him in the garage. He was beyond curious. The moment they were out of sight, Mickey spun on him. Before he saw it coming, Mickey's hand was around his throat and Edge's back hit the wall. He didn't get a chance for the rage to hit. Mickey's' mouth covered his. Edge forgot how to breathe. His knees weakened. Thankfully, Mickey still held him by the throat, keeping him upright. It was arguably the hottest kiss of his life, especially considering it was with his biggest obsession.

Mickey pulled away. He looked turned on. Edge couldn't look away. He knew the image would burn into his brain. "You did great today. Your pre-planning saved everyone."

Without another word, Mickey walked away, leaving Edge panting and slightly confused. He certainly hadn't seen that coming. Edge wasn't disappointed.

Chapter Two

SWEAT ROLLED DOWN MICKEY'S back. He tried like hell to stay focused on his breathing and nothing else. Climbing that building had made him realize he had neglected his pull-ups for too long. While he had pulled off the climb, it hadn't been as easy as it used to be. The way Edge scaled the wall had shown him his shortcomings. Granted, Edge was tall and lanky. He had less weight to carry up a vertical surface, but Edge had been sleeveless the day he had abducted Mickey and Mickey had seen how cut and thick those arms were. Muscle wasn't light. Mickey needed to work harder.

"Do you think if I stopped dancing, I'd get fat?"

Mickey dropped from the bar to focus on Kylo at the question. He sat nearby on the floor with his snacks and coloring books. "No. You have too lean of a build."

Kylo nodded, but he didn't look up. "Do you think Beau would still love me if I got fat?"

Kylo didn't sound quite right. These questions weren't like him. "I think Beau would love you even if he had to wheel you around in a wheelbarrow. Why?"

Kylo shrugged. "I don't know. Other than a couple of hours yesterday, I haven't seen him a lot lately. He's always gone when I wake up and I'm asleep before he comes to bed. I was just sitting here thinking that I feel fat, so maybe I'm fat." He shrugged again. "Nothing feels right."

His arms were beet red. Something was definitely wrong. "Look at me, sweetie."

Kylo's chin lifted. His face was swollen and red. All the alarms bells rang. He knew that look. "Can you breathe okay?"

Kylo visibly tried to swallow. "I don't know." He made a sound like sucking air through a straw and Mickey flew into action. In a flash, he had Kylo over his shoulder at a full run down the hall with his phone to his ear.

"What's wrong?" Beau knew Mickey wouldn't call his emergency phone from upstairs unless it truly was an emergency. "My room. Now. Kylo isn't breathing." He knew he was vague and maybe dramatic, but he needed Beau to get their family physician there. Mickey was about to hit Kylo with an EpiPen. He would still need medical care afterward... if it worked. God, it had to work.

He dumped a visibly panicked Kylo on his bed and ran for the bathroom. Mickey easily found one of his spare EpiPens and was back in a flash. Without an ounce of hesitation, he stabbed Kylo in the thigh.

Almost immediately, even though it felt like it took forever, he heard Kylo take a breath. It was still labored, but then he took another.

Beau burst into the room with Henry hot on his heels. He was on the bed before Mickey could say a word. "Holy shit. What happened?"

Mickey was out of breath from the sheer terror. "I don't know. He had an allergic reaction, but I don't know why. One second, he was coloring, and the next, he was all red in the face and fighting for air."

"Austen is on the way," Henry said, holding the phone to his ear.

Mickey nodded. He couldn't look at anyone but Kylo. If the swelling didn't subside, he might need another shot. Mickey wasn't above that if it kept Kylo breathing.

"Did something sting him? Did he eat something new? I don't understand." Beau sounded every bit as panicked as Mickey felt.

Mickey just babbled, trying to make his brain work. "I don't know. He asked if I thought you'd still love him if he got fat. Then he said something about never seeing you anymore, then he wasn't breathing. I don't know." Mickey had always been good under pressure. This was different. It was Kylo. Maybe it was his job to watch Kylo, but they spent nearly every waking moment together. He was Mickey's best friend. He was amazing and Mickey couldn't handle anything happening to him.

Henry grabbed him from behind and squeezed, shoring him up. Mickey leaned into him and tried to clear his head. He swiped his hand over his eyes. "Um. Let me think. He wanted milk and cookies, but we were out of milk. Chef Fabrice said there was soy milk, but it was Clay's since he's allergic to milk. Clay was in the kitchen, and he said it was okay if Kylo wanted it. Kylo said he'd never tried soy milk, but he wasn't opposed. So, I guess that's new, but it's soy milk. That's what people drink when they're allergic to milk."

"Soybeans are a very common allergy. In fact, it's one of the big eight that can cause severe reactions."

Mickey sagged in relief as Austen strolled into the room, sounding calm and spouting facts.

He was at Kylo's side and working in no time.

Henry squeezed his shoulders. "Go take a walk. You need a minute."

Mickey nodded. It felt like his brain rattled in his head. He had never been more scared, and he worked for a fucking crime lord. Mickey headed downstairs on autopilot. He needed to go to the store and get milk. That was what he should have done this morning. If he had, Kylo would be okay.

Rain appeared in his path. "Is he okay?"

Mickey didn't have the strength to calm anyone else. Austen's husband was one of Kylo's oldest friends. Mickey motioned toward the stairs. "Second floor on the left. Second to the last door at the end of the hall."

Rain ran for the stairs.

Mickey made his way to the garage. That was where he found Edge waiting. Their gazes met and didn't budge.

Edge made a helpless gesture. "I drove Rain and Austen."

That made sense. Rain was part of his team. They all lived together. Rain was probably too close to the situation to drive. He didn't know why Austen couldn't. Mickey gave a jerky nod. His throat wouldn't work.

"He'll be okay. Austen says he keeps you stocked with EpiPens, and you'd know what to do. I take it you have some sort of severe allergy?"

Mickey's hands rose and fell. He couldn't hold a conversation right now. "Peanuts."

Edge nodded. "You should probably steer clear of Field, then. I'm pretty sure ninety-nine percent of his diet consists of peanut butter."

"I need to get Kylo some milk."

Edge motioned toward the Dodge Challenger he leaned against. "I'll take you. You don't look like you need to be driving."

He was so calm. In control. Just like he had been on that rooftop, Edge was a born caretaker and leader. He made it hard to panic.

Mickey headed for the car when Edge opened the passenger door for him. Before he could climb inside, Edge was in his space. His mouth covered Mickey's and air finally filled his lungs fully since Kylo stopped breathing.

Edge pulled away. "Now you can get in, sexy."

Mickey didn't respond. He simply climbed into the car and accepted his fate. Edge was in control. Mickey was just along for the ride.

If Edge understood anything, it was the look of a man who had almost lost someone in their charge. Duty was all Edge had. Keeping his brothers safe was everything. Without them, he was nothing. Edge had failed before and wouldn't again. Mickey hadn't failed, but the attack had been unexpected and he was still in shock. He didn't even realize he was shirtless until Edge pulled into the parking lot of the grocery store and pointed it out.

"What kind of milk does he need? I'll get it. I'm pretty sure no shoes, no shirt, no service is still a thing."

Mickey glanced down at himself. "Oh. Damn. Sorry. I was in the middle of my workout."

Edge had zero complaints. He had known the body beneath the guy's clothes would be amazing. Edge hadn't been wrong.

Mickey shifted positions as if to dig out his wallet. "Well, fuck. I guess the milk will have to wait."

He looked so adorably defeated at the realization he didn't have his wallet. Likely he would have noticed before leaving—since he didn't seem to have any keys either—if Edge hadn't talked him into getting into his car.

"You're good. I've got it."

Mickey's shoulders sank lower. "Thanks. I'll pay you back when we get home. Um." He scrubbed his hand across his eyes. "Kylo drinks whole milk."

With a wink, Edge climbed from the car and made his way inside. It took less than five minutes to grab a gallon and be right back outside with Mickey. Still, Edge resented the time lost. Thankfully, Mickey seemed to have recovered a bit as Edge passed the milk his way.

"How much do I owe you?"

Edge shrugged. "It's on me. You can buy me a drink sometime."

"All right."

His easy agreement bolstered Edge's hopes. After their kiss, Edge had immediately begun questioning every moment and second-guessing everything. There was no reason for Mickey to see him again. It was a kiss. Kisses meant nothing to most people. Edge should forget it. He couldn't.

Unfortunately, the silence that followed wasn't as comfortable as he liked. He found himself needing to fill it. "So..." He tapped his fingers on the steering wheel as he drove. "What kind of workout do you do?"

"Actually, I decided to work on my upper body strength today. After scaling that building, I realized how much I've been neglecting pull-ups."

Edge couldn't help but smile. "You didn't look like you struggled."

"I can always be better. Just because I don't go on jobs with Beau anymore doesn't mean I should let anything slip. Anyone who sees Beau with Kylo knows Kylo is his weakness. If anything, I'm probably more in danger now that it's my job to stick to him. Not that I'm complaining."

Of course he wasn't. Edge got the feeling Mickey never complained. "Well, you said you grew up homeless, so I doubt you feel like you're allowed to be unhappy now."

"Oof. You said you grew up abused. Do you want to drag that out too?"

Edge couldn't stop smiling. Even the heavy topic didn't dim his mood. "I mean, if you want. Honestly, I'd be shocked if you didn't already know all about me. Between being friends with

Kylo and Beau having us all investigated—I'm sure—you probably know more about me than I do."

"Be shocked, then. Kylo doesn't talk about any of you beyond your present friendship. If Beau had you investigated, and he likely did, he didn't share any of that info with me. I'm just a foot soldier."

Edge tossed Mickey a look of disbelief. "I highly doubt that. Beau wouldn't trust just anyone with Kylo. You're a lot higher in those ranks than you think. I'd go as far to say you're right under Henry, if not equal to him."

Mickey laughed. "Don't let that fool you into thinking I know a damn thing going on in Beau's business. He's always been the type to move in complete silence. That's what makes him so fucking terrifying. Well, one thing."

Edge nodded. "I can imagine. People like him don't live as long as he has without being genius levels ahead of everyone."

"I have a feeling that you're also describing yourself."

A snort burst from Edge before he could stop it. "I don't know about all that."

"How long have you kept your bunch alive, hidden, and out of prison?"

"Yeah. I'm not doing that alone. It's a team effort. Everyone plays their role. We all stay safe. Why do you think Austen moved in with us rather than Rain moving in with him? If we don't stick together, everything we've built will fall to pieces. I recognize that sounds dramatic, but that's just how it is. We'll be hunted until the end of our days. If we split, they'll pick us off one by one. Only together are we a force they won't dare cross."

"Who is we?"

Edge had forgotten he spoke to someone who didn't know him. He was so accustomed to being surrounded by only his brothers that he hadn't watched his words. Not that it mattered. "The Russian government."

Mickey didn't react right away. When he did, he did so in the funniest way possible, in Edge's opinion. "Yeah. That's a lot of people."

A bark of laughter escaped Edge. He genuinely liked Mickey. Unfortunately, their time was over too soon. The moment they pulled into the garage, Henry damn near ripped the passenger door off his car. "I tried calling. Where in the hell have you been?"

Mickey leapt from the car like his ass was on fire. "I got Kylo's milk. I forgot my phone. Is everything okay? Is Kylo all right?"

Henry ran his fingers through his hair. It was the most shaken Edge had ever seen the guy, including Edge bringing Mickey home from Mexico. "Yeah. Sorry. I didn't think about you not having your phone." His gaze slid down Mickey's body. "It looks like you forgot a few things."

"Not the milk." He waved the jug.

Henry automatically lit, becoming someone new. "I see that." His eyes sparkled with laughter. "When Kylo's up and moving, and Beau lets him leave the bed again, I'm sure Kylo will be grateful." His gaze slid down Mickey's body again. "Where is all your stuff? You're not even armed. You know better than that."

Edge whipped a gun from a holster at his waist. "He was good. I had his back."

Henry's gaze moved from the weapon to Edge. He dipped his chin. "Thanks for that."

Mickey made another awkward motion with the milk. "I should put this away and grab my shit from the gym." He focused on Edge. "Thank you."

Edge dipped his chin. He desperately wanted to find a way to stay in Mickey's company, but Rain appeared, stealing his chance. "Hey. Can you take me home so I can pick up my car and pack a bag for Austen and me? We need to stay the night in case Kylo needs us. Well, Austen. I'm pretty useless in this scenario."

He recognized Rain tried to lighten the mood, but all Edge felt was longing. For years, he had avoided all attachments. Now here was this guy and everything stood in their way, especially Edge's inability to simply reach for what he wanted. But Edge would be back, and he would keep trying. He hadn't been this invested in a long time. The time had come for him to try to move on from things that would never be.

Chapter Three

UNKNOWN NUMBER: *It's Mickey. I hope you don't mind, but I got your number from Rain. Do you want to go do something tonight? Beau is making Kylo stay in bed while he hovers like a worried mom. So I'm free and bored.*

Unknown number: *Not that I'm only asking because I'm bored. I realized how that sounded as soon as I hit send.*

Edge: *Just saved your number to my phone, and I'd love to do something. What did you have in mind?*

Mickey: *LOL! I kind of hoped you'd have a suggestion since I never do things.*

Edge: *And you think I do? It's Saturday night and I'm sitting here with a book. That's what I do.*

Mickey: *Oh. Well, what are you reading?*

Edge: *I'm open to doing something other than reading.*

Edge: *Did I lose you?*

Mickey: *Sorry. I went to ask Rain what people do? *awkward laugh* He said if we haven't had dinner, we could do that.*

Edge: *Oh no. I just ordered dinner. Would you like to come over and share? I got something I always split into two meals anyhow.*

Mickey: *Sounds great. I'll be there soon.*

Edge: *Great. See you then.*

Mickey had no idea why he was nervous. That wasn't a feeling he usually suffered. He would like to think he was a confident guy. But Mickey didn't really date, so this was unfamiliar territory for him. His job didn't allow for relationships. Partners were a vulnerability. Edge could take care of himself. Still, Mickey had no idea why he was here.

He rang the doorbell and tried to look nonchalant. When Edge answered, all discomfort fell away. He held up the book he had brought.

"We can read together."

The smile Edge had worn opening the door grew bigger. He stepped back, making room for Mickey to pass. "Is that really what you want to do?"

Mickey shrugged. "I'm about halfway through. Reading is my usual Saturday night too. After Beau is finished working for the night, anyhow."

"I'm a little more than halfway through my book. We could swap when we get finished." He motioned for Mickey to follow. "Our food just got here. I have us set up in my room so we can eat in peace. There's always someone coming and going around here." He headed down the hall, still speaking over his shoulder as he went. "The kitchen and living room are basically the only common areas around here. If you're in either room, you're fair game for Field's antics." They passed several closed doors. Everything looked high dollar, but Mickey was used to that and Edge was more interesting. "We each have our own space to get away." He opened a door, and they were in what looked like an upscale hotel room. There was a sitting room and a mini kitchen. He didn't see a place to eat other than the small settee.

Mickey looked around while Edge kept moving and talking. He grabbed a bag from the microwave and found a couple of plates. "Luckily, you were right behind the food, so I don't have to reheat anything. Do you like Mexican? I always get this huge chicken and rice bowl thing." He showed it to Mickey before he divided it onto two plates.

"Oh. I love that place. It's..." He searched his mind but couldn't think of the name.

"It's on the corner of Maple and Main, right?"

Edge flashed him a smile and passed him a plate. "Yeah. I hope you don't mind eating on the bed. Everyone else has their own table and all that, but I usually just eat in bed. I keep the place clean, and—honestly—it's less depressing than sitting at a table alone."

A legitimate reason to get Edge in bed? He was in. "That's cool. If I can't eat dinner with Henry, I usually take my food to my room too. If I have to sit alone, I'd rather do it in front of the TV."

"Exactly." Edge opened the mini wine fridge. "I have wine, beer, and Coke."

"Whatever you're having is fine."

Edge pulled a Coke from the fridge and passed it Mickey's way before grabbing one for himself. Together, they headed for the bed. Mickey sat on one side, using the nightstand as a table for his book and drink. Edge did the same on the other. They ate in companionable silence for a few minutes.

Mickey finally broke it. "Thank you for dinner and for keeping me company."

Edge looked his way. "I'm glad you reached out." He looked serious.

Mickey felt things. He set his plate on the table and grabbed his drink. Mickey sipped while he waited for Edge to finish. He had always been a fast eater.

It felt like it took forever before Edge finally set his plate aside and chugged his drink. The moment Edge's hands were free, Mickey rolled to his knees. With one quick tug, he had Edge dragged beneath him.

Laughter swam in Edge's gorgeous brown eyes. "You're entirely too comfortable manhandling me."

Mickey ran his hand up Edge's side, slipping beneath his shirt. He massaged the first hint of bare skin he reached. "Is this you lodging a formal complaint?"

Edge held his stare. His gaze turned heated. "I'm unsure. I'm used to being the one in control. Around here, anyhow, since I don't know shit about relationships, I guess I'm okay with you being in charge."

He said relationships and Mickey didn't know how he felt about that. Still, he didn't argue. "I'm not in control. Not in the least." In fact, Mickey had never been more out of control in his life. That didn't stop him from lowering his head and taking the kiss he wanted, like he had any idea what he was doing here. Mickey didn't know shit about how to make or keep anyone happy. All he knew was Edge looked at him in a hungry way no one ever had, and he had to know how that translated into the bedroom. He needed that obsession unleashed on him. Mickey was tired of watching everyone around him find love or just—he didn't know. People just seemed to enjoy life in a way he never had. Mickey wanted to feel.

Edge pushed, urging Mickey onto his back. "If you're not in charge, then I want to be." He straddled Mickey and took the exact kiss Mickey expected from Edge based solely on the way he ate Mickey alive with his stare.

The instant, all-consuming desire that hit Mickey would have taken him to his knees if he had been standing. But Mickey still kept his touch respectful, even as Edge tried to steal his soul. He didn't know where to put his hands, so he just wrapped his arms around Edge and hung on. Mickey couldn't deny he was turned on and definitely wanted more. It was good Edge wanted to lead. Mickey didn't know where he was going.

Edge suddenly rolled to his side. He stayed cuddled close with his leg thrown over Mickey's body.

"So, what book did you bring?"

Mickey fought to grab a thought. His body screamed and he couldn't catch his breath. "Um. It's a murder mystery." For the life of him, he couldn't think of the title. Edge had him a mess. "What are you reading?"

Sexy eyes focused on him. "Whoa. You really are willing to just stop and read if that's what I want to do."

Edge confused him more and more by the second. "What else would I do?"

"Jesus." Edge's whispered open surprise only baffled Mickey more. "Where did Beau find you?"

Aggravation set in. Edge was strange. He didn't understand what the guy wanted from him. "From an alley. Are you questioning my worth?" His irritation turned to anger. "Look, I don't know what I did to make you think I'm not good enough to do my job, but—"

Edge straddled his body and had his tongue in Mickey's mouth again before he even saw it coming. Part of him wanted to shove Edge away. He didn't like it when people tried to play him for the fun of it. Unfortunately, he liked Edge's kiss too much. He didn't fight.

"I think you're perfect." Edge's whispered claim between kisses had Mickey's muscles relaxing. He still didn't know what in the hell was going on, but he also wasn't ready to leave.

The way Mickey had just been ready to accept Edge's kiss and stop there had Edge floored. It had been a test. Was it fair? No, but Edge had been through hell and survived evil. He wouldn't willingly step into Hell again. Edge knew he confounded Mickey, and the poor guy was probably ready to just walk away. But Mickey was adorably unaware of his worth and Edge wanted to be the one who showed him the truth. He was as beautiful on the inside as he was on the outside. That was so incredibly rare.

Edge loved Mickey's mouth. The guy kissed like he was starved of affection. Maybe he was. It wasn't like either of them were in a position to have normal relationships.

Mickey's hands finally moved from lightly holding Edge's waist to his ass. He moved in an unsure way that only had the mystery of him growing. The first time Mickey had kissed him, he had done so like a boss. Even tonight, that first kiss had been with all the confidence. Since he ended up beneath Edge, he had turned awkward and unsure. Edge wondered if he had never let anyone else take the lead before. It was kind of hot, thinking he was the first.

Edge's mouth moved to Mickey's neck. The sound of Mickey's ragged breathing fed his lust. Edge pushed Mickey's shirt up his torso. He wanted to have Mickey shirtless again, especially since he was touching him this time. To his surprise, Mickey used the strength of his core to roll slightly upward and whip his shirt over his head. As he tossed it aside, Edge peeled off his shirt and then went back to exploring Mickey's body with his mouth. Mickey's hands moved back to Edge's waist as if he wanted to touch bare skin. Then his fingers traced the line of Edge's jeans until he reached the button. He went to work, sliding it loose before pulling the zipper down. Edge kept his weight on his knees, so Mickey had room to work. Unfortunately, that was where he stopped. It was as if they were taking turns pushing past boundaries. Edge sat back on his heels and went to work on the front of Mickey's jeans. Mickey breathed hard, as if he had run a marathon and stopped for a break. He looked sexy as fuck and turned on. Edge didn't know where to look. Everything about him called for Edge's inspection. Then he had Mickey's erection free. He had a really nice dick. Edge was kind of a mess of desperation, but he didn't want to show it.

"You should take off your pants." At Mickey's rough-sounding words, as if he had been eating gravel, Edge realized this was real. They were together. This would happen. The moment felt surreal for some reason, as if he had stepped outside himself and let a stranger take over.

"How exactly do you see this going?" He hated to ruin the mood and pace, but they didn't know each other. Not really. Mickey was a lot more dominating than Edge expected. While there was nothing Edge hadn't done, he definitely had his preferences, and he had a bad feeling Mickey's were the same. Either way, Edge was still in.

Mickey didn't look the least bit taken out of the moment. In fact, he looked twice as aroused, as if communication was his kink. "Honestly. I don't even understand it myself, but I really want you to fuck me."

Damn. It was just as Edge thought. Mickey wasn't a bottom, but he wanted that with Edge. That was a lot of trust and that was exactly what Edge needed. His past was ugly. It had been made much uglier by falling in love with a different blond-haired and green-eyed beauty. That love had been a weakness that nearly destroyed his mind. He didn't know if he could let go of control again. Not completely, anyhow. There were so many things he didn't know if he was ready for with Mickey, but this—this he could do.

Edge stroked Mickey's cock, keeping him in the moment. "If you decide you don't want this, just say so. There are so many ways I can make you fly. If you get uncomfortable, say the word."

"I'm not worried."

Damn. He was beautiful. Edge climbed from the bed and stripped while Mickey watched. Once nude, he opened the bedside drawer and grabbed the lube and a condom. Mickey scrambled his way out of his pants at the sight.

Edge bit back a smile. He couldn't say Mickey didn't know what he wanted. The moment he was back on the bed, Edge positioned himself between Mickey's thighs. While sitting back on his heels, he opened the lube. "I'm going to talk through everything I do."

Mickey's sexy green eyes never wavered from him. The flush across the bridge of his nose and cheeks made the green pop. Edge was hooked. There was a sickness inside him even he didn't want to look at too closely. Memories wanted to float to the surface and choke him. He wasn't a prisoner any longer. No one would punish him for this obsession.

With his fingers thoroughly soaked, he circled Mickey's asshole, wetting him and getting ready to stretch him.

"Why me?" The question popped from Edge with zero good sense or permission from his brain. It was like he wanted to ruin the night. He didn't expect Mickey would answer.

Mickey shocked him with his quick response. "Because of how you're looking at me right now."

Edge didn't need him to expound. He knew exactly how he looked at Mickey. There was no hiding the sick level of desire that choked him every time he stared at Mickey. Only having him would ease the gnawing at his gut. Unfortunately, as he slipped one finger inside Mickey, he feared for what was left of his sanity as he realized having him wouldn't be enough. He was more frightened of himself than he had ever been, and that should terrify Mickey.

Edge curled his finger. He knew he hit the right spot by the way Mickey turned twice as sexy. He swallowed air—like a drowning man.

"When I'm inside you, this is my goal. I want to see when I'm at this perfect angle, hitting this exact spot." He worked a second finger inside and then a third. Edge did his best to ease Mickey into things. He didn't put on his condom until he was certain Mickey could take him. "If I'm not giving you exactly what you need, say so. I only want to make you feel good."

He was so quiet. So accepting.

Edge needed to hear Mickey's pleasure. He led his cock to Mickey's asshole. Edge studied his every reaction, backing off when he thought he might be hurting him and pushing forward when Mickey looked ready for more. The guy was so fucking tight, he had sweat coating Edge's skin while he called on every ounce of patience he possessed. Thankfully, years of waiting for the perfect shot and planning missions in minute detail had him prepared for the task. Edge knew the instant he hit that sweet spot.

A sexy low moan escaped Mickey. "Yes. Like that."

Oh, fuck. He nearly came at the neediness in Mickey's voice. Edge drew a shaky breath as he made some shallow pumps, hitting where Mickey needed him while also trying to slow the oncoming orgasm. Mickey had him weak.

"You've got me dangerously close to disappointing you."

Before Edge saw it coming, Mickey snagged his hair and hauled him forward. "Then blow. I know you'll make me come one way or another." His tongue shoved its way into Edge's mouth and Edge was gone. He forgot everything but the way Mickey felt on his dick and the animalistic way he kissed. Edge felt devoured in a way he couldn't explain. It was like Mickey stole his soul. In two thrusts, he was crying out and shaking in Mickey's arms. His whole body jerked with the power of his orgasm. He made sounds he never had. The pleasure dancing on his cock was like heroin. Edge already knew he would beg for more. The moment he regained an ounce of sense, Edge had to make Mickey feel every bit as good. Pride demanded Mickey lose himself every bit as much as Edge had. He didn't waste a second. Edge was down Mickey's body with Mickey's dick in his mouth before an ounce of sweat cooled. Mickey writhed beneath him. He moaned, begged, and babbled things even Edge couldn't understand. His muscles clenched and Edge swallowed Mickey's cock. Mickey's body nearly jackknifed from the bed as he jerked hard enough to pull a muscle. He cried out as Edge drank every drop of cum Mickey gave him. Then, somehow, they were a tangle of sweaty arms and legs as their tongues played. A surge of happiness ran through him and settled into his chest. His eyes burned. Edge found something in Mickey's arms that he thought he had lost a long time ago. He needed more than just one night.

Chapter Four

IT WAS ODD NOT having Kylo nearby while going through his daily workout. Mickey had gotten accustomed to his happy nonstop chatter. Today, he was a little grateful for the silence, because his mind was loud as hell. He kept playing through his night with Edge. Mickey realized he should feel some sort of way about how Edge made him someone he wasn't, but all he could think was maybe he was that guy... or not. Maybe it was just Edge. Possibly Mickey had been alone and unseen too long. Hell, he didn't know. All Mickey knew was the night had been hot as fuck, and he definitely wanted to go again. He got hard every time he thought about it. It took everything Mickey had not to text the guy and make plans. His pride stopped him. They had left off with a sexy good-bye kiss, and now Mickey had to wait. He couldn't go crawling back for more. That just wasn't him. Goddamn. It was killing him.

Mickey didn't make it through his shower without jacking off to the memory. He kind of hated that the same dude who had once had a gun to his head was now the guy Mickey craved with every fiber of his being. Mickey comforted himself that Edge had sucked his dick, so maybe they were even now. Still, he had to get his head back in the game. Kylo was still in bed and Mickey needed to figure out what his day would look like with nothing to do. He dressed and made his way downstairs.

Henry met him at the bottom of the stairs. He handed Mickey a breakfast sandwich from his favorite fast-food restaurant and a cup of coffee. "You've been reassigned for a while. Let's go. You're with me today."

Mickey's mind went numb. "Is the food to lessen the blow of Kylo hating me now?"

A deep line appeared between Henry's light brown eyes. "What? Kylo doesn't hate you. He doesn't blame you at all. He's just not better today. Beau is determined to stay glued to him. But it seems he's completely covered in hives today, so Beau is still worried."

"Hives? Why? What does Austen say?"

Henry headed for the garage and answered over his shoulder as he went. "He thinks this allergic reaction might have uncovered an autoimmune disease. Don't worry. You know he has the best care in the country. He'll be fine. In a way, this is a good thing. Don't repeat that." He waited until they were in the SUV before explaining. "Beau's been so caught up in the weird shit going on in Mexico for so long now, it's hurting their relationship. It's time he stepped back for a minute. This gave him the excuse."

That was true. As long as Kylo was okay and didn't hate him, then Mickey could handle a change in duties. "Where are we headed?"

"To check out the Agafonov boys."

Mickey took a sip of his coffee to hide his immediate reaction. The drink was doctored perfectly. Henry spent too much time with him. They knew each other too well. The moment of swallowing gave him the chance to get his heart rate under control. His voice sounded oddly normal when he spoke. "What brought on this errand?" He ate, pretending like the answer meant nothing to him.

Henry kept his gaze on the road. "Rumor is, the reason Beau got betrayed is because there's a new player in town. He undercut Beau, but the only way Miquel could break his deal with Beau was to permanently remove Beau from the board. Obviously, he knows he'll turn up dead for reneging on their bargain. The thing is, now we know all the players and what's happening. Beau is fine with stepping back from Mexico. In fact, you didn't hear this, but he's thinking of retiring completely after learning Kylo thought he was done with him."

That genuinely surprised Mickey. Then again, he had never seen Beau love anyone the way he did Kylo, so maybe it wasn't that shocking.

Henry kept going. "Anyhow, he obviously can't just let the whole Mexico incident go. Retired or not, he can't look weak. That would endanger us all. So, he put out a rumor that he's having supply chain issues and that's why he wasn't there to meet with Miguel, freeing Miguel to meet with this person who tried to get us all taken out. We know when and where they're meeting."

Mickey saw the plan come together. "In comes the Agafonov crew to take them out while they're in one place."

Henry nodded. "Exactly. With everyone removed from the playing field in Mexico, Beau can walk away. New people will eventually step up and he'll be old news. One area shut down and more time freed for Kylo. Plus, that's just become a shit show and too far to travel for too little money and too high of risk. It's not like Beau can do this forever."

"It's not like any of us need the money," Mickey said, adding his two cents.

Henry flashed him a smile. "Exactly." He headed into an area where Mickey never went. Mostly since it was just office buildings and places not open to the general public. Mickey spotted Edge's car before he saw the huge black van. The realization had him fighting a chuckle. He had really gotten a little crazy about the guy. Austen's SUV sat parked next to the van. All three vehicles sat outside a red brick building. There were no signs explaining what the business was. The windows were blacked out. Henry parked on the other side of Austen, and they headed for the door together. There was a trash can right outside the door. Mickey paused to toss his empty coffee cup and sandwich wrapper inside before following Henry through the door. It was a dance studio.

Mickey's feet slowed at the sight that met him. Tracker had an entire area set up that almost looked like a DJ booth, except it was nothing but computer components and monitors. A few small tables scattered around the outside of the dance floor where some of the guys sat together, staring and scrolling through something on a tablet. They never even looked Henry and Mickey's way. In the center of the dance floor, back-to-back, Rain was in all white while Shadow wore all black. They each wore virtual reality glasses. They moved perfectly in sync. Whatever Rain did, Shadow did in reverse. It was obvious they navigated their way through whatever they saw inside their glasses. Shadow bent over backwards, staying perfectly glued and mimicking every move. It was one of the coolest things he had ever seen. They would have zero blind spots together.

An alarm blared. "Fuck!" The pair straightened but stayed back-to-back. "That was my fault," Rain yelled. "Restart from the beginning."

They went back to walking in place and matching each other moves. It was al- most like a dance. Rain was blond and light, Shadow was dark. They were the same size. Almost identical. It was wild to watch. Then he spotted Edge. Everything disappeared.

The alarm blared again. "Goddamn it. It was me that time. Sorry, Rain."

Mickey heard Shadow speaking, but he was too busy staring at the sexy man headed his way. Damn, the way he moved made it hard to breathe. It was that confident swagger that had Mickey begging to be beneath him. This entire situation was nuts.

Edge's gorgeous smile made an appearance. His gaze moved between Mickey and Henry. "Hey. Sorry about the noise. Day one is always the roughest. The guys are still learning the schematics."

Henry nodded, looking as if he barely listened as he watched the pair on the dance floor. In unison, knives appeared in the men's hands. "That's really amazing."

Edge glanced behind him. "Yeah. They've had well over a decade of practice. Between this and performing together on stage, they're damn near perfect together. It won't take them long to have the entire operation memorized step by step. Your boss will get his money's worth."

"How do you prepare for contingencies? It's one thing to memorize the building and guess at where guards will be, but what if something is inevitably out of place or goes wrong?"

At Henry's question, Edge shrugged. "That's where I come in, and Ridge, of course. We'll be positioned on nearby rooftops with a clear view through our scopes." He pointed toward where Field sat with Shore. "If there's an angle we can't see, then those two will have the ground covered." Field looked serious in a way Mickey hadn't seen. While he had glanced Henry's way once, he went right back to work.

Edge kept up the explanation. "Tracker will have the entire building wired for video and sound. There won't be a thing he can't see. If—for whatever reason—none of us snipers can get a clear shot, then Scout will come in for up close rapid fire. He's the best in the world at hitting targets with total accuracy at a high rate of speed. Tidy and Crisp aren't here, since they're not needed for this part, but they come in behind us and ensure no one ever knows we were there. In this case, the bodies will be left behind, of course. Everyone will know what happens when Beau is crossed."

"Do you care if I check out what everyone is doing?"

Edge waved toward the room in general at Henry's question. "Knock yourself out. Beau is paying us, after all. You're entitled to see how it'll come together." Edge focused on him. "I have that book for you we talked about."

"Great."

They both sounded so nonchalant—like barely acquaintances.

"It's in my car if you'd like to come with me to grab it."

Henry glanced his way for half a second, but didn't look suspicious. He knew Mickey liked to read.

"Sure. I'll be right back, Henry."

"All right." He moved toward the booth where Tracker watched the monitors.

Mickey fell into step with Edge on the way to the door.

"You forgot your book at my place." Edge didn't look his way as he spoke. "It really is in my car." He opened the door for Mickey and didn't speak again until they were alone. "I just wanted an excuse to have you alone." He made the claim over his shoulder as he made his way out of sight to where his car was parked. The van hid him.

Mickey followed like Edge had magnetized his dick.

The second they were out of sight of the door, Edge backed him against the van.

"I thought about using the book as an excuse to see you again tonight."

Mickey's hands automatically slid across Edge's hips. He drew the man closer. "You don't need an excuse for that. All you have to do is ask."

A gorgeous smile touched Edge's lips. It was filled with humor. "Do you want to come over and make out tonight?"

Mickey felt how big he smiled, but he couldn't stop. "Yeah. I want that." His smile slipped away as the final inch between them disappeared. Their lips met. It wasn't the hungry kisses they shared last night. This one was sexy and made Mickey feel something he couldn't explain. Of course, he had been confused for a while now. This was different. When their lips parted, they froze for a second and shared air before their tongues met. It was one of the most powerful moments of his life and Mickey couldn't explain that either. The experience was beyond description. It was felt. Then he heard the door open.

Like lightning, Edge was inside his car and back out with Mickey's book in hand. Henry appeared just as Mickey turned in that direction. His gaze moved between them.

Mickey awkwardly held up the book for a second. "Got it."

While Henry looked slightly confused, he didn't question him. "Come on. You should see what they've put together. Their virtual program is pretty amazing."

Mickey nodded and followed Henry like nothing had happened. It wasn't that he was ashamed or hiding anything. Mickey just wasn't ready to share something that might just be a fling or whatever. Plus, it wasn't like he knew anything about Henry's personal life. They had never gotten into each other's business like that. So, for now, he would just see where things went. Neither of them was truly free to have a normal relationship. This was likely all they would ever be.

Goddamn. Mickey was sexy. His blond hair was shaggy and curled at the ends as it brushed his collar. The guy's wide shoulders made him want to lick him.

He was just this solid wall of tight muscles and sexy confidence. Jesus, it was hard as hell to stay professional, but Henry was Mickey's boss and Henry's boss had hired them for a job. He had to pretend Mickey hadn't made him blow so fast last night, he should be embarrassed. Edge wasn't. He had gotten Mickey off pretty fucking quickly too. A smirk pulled at his lips. Then they had slowed things down. By that second orgasm, they had both been covered in sweat and begging for relief. Edge desperately needed to do it again.

Field sat in the booth with Tracker, as if he knew Henry would be back. They piled in too. Tracker immediately jumped in, pointing their attention toward the screens that showed what Rain and Shadow saw. "Here's how the boys train."

Field wasn't one to be ignored for long. "Are you two coming to my birthday party tonight?"

Mickey looked slightly taken aback. "Uh. Sure. I guess."

Tracker shot Edge a knowing look and horror set in. He had forgotten the entire place was wired, and the monitors were inside Tracker's booth. He had to have seen and heard everything. Worse than that, Henry had been with Tracker while they were outside. Tracker made a subtle move so Edge could see the screen that showed the parking lot was black. He clicked a key and brought the camera back online. Relief flooded through Edge.

Field kept Henry distracted. "What about you, sexy daddy? Will you come celebrate all over me? The party is at seven at our place."

Henry never looked away from the mission. "How old are you now? Sixteen?"

Field didn't let Henry's disinterest deter him. After all, this version of Field was just a mask. "Close. Twenty-nine. I'm of age."

Edge rolled his eyes.

Mickey tossed him a laughing smile, obviously enjoying the way Field always toyed with Henry.

Henry looked his way, forcing Edge to hide his facial expression. "This is great. Thank you for letting us see behind the scenes. Beau will be glad to hear how hard you're working." He glanced toward Mickey. "Let's go."

Mickey nodded. He looked serious, obviously being the professional. When Henry turned his back, Mickey tossed him one more heated glance before following Henry out.

"Damn, Edge. I've never seen you smile this much and mean it." Tracker's observation chafed, but it was true. It was Tracker's job to see everything. He couldn't hide. "Thanks for pulling that feed. I forgot about that camera, and I gather Henry expects complete focus and professionalism at all times."

"I wonder what it must be like to have a boss like that?" Field said the words in a mocking tone, obviously taking a jab at how stiff Edge was all the time.

"I'm not your boss."

Tracker and Field exchanged a glance at Edge's claim. They burst into laughter. "Get back to work." He walked away before they got under his skin.

"He's not our boss," they said simultaneously, laughing.

Edge didn't look back. He knew he could be bossy sometimes, and he was considered the leader of the group. Jesus. He was their boss. Edge pulled out his phone. He needed to talk to someone he didn't consider a brother.

Edge: *If you felt put on the spot, you don't have to come tonight.*

Mickey: *Do you want me to come?*

He wanted to say no and hang on to his pride. The least Edge could do was give the guy an out. After all, that was why he had texted in the first place.

Edge: *Yes.*

Well, fuck.

Mickey: *Then I'll be there. What should I get Field?*

Edge: *That's a tough one. He has every-thing. You don't have to bring a gift, though. Field will just be grateful you showed. Outside our group, he doesn't have any friends. He's a little too intense for people.*

Mickey: *I have a hard time picturing that. It seems like he'd always be the life of the party. Nonetheless, I'll think of something and see you at seven.*

Edge: *See you then.*

Seven couldn't get here fast enough. Field wasn't the only one who need-ed something outside his brothers. He could let Mickey fill him way too easily.

His cup had been empty too long. Edge
had to be careful.

Chapter Five

As billed, Mickey didn't see any cars when he arrived. Everyone who lived there usually kept their cars in the garage. That likely meant no one else outside the family was there. He had thought about Edge's texts way more than he should. The longer he mulled things over, the more Edge's confessions made sense. He honestly couldn't see Field acting the way he did around Henry for all hours of the day. There was something behind his eyes when he was obnoxious—like he purposely made people uncomfortable so they wouldn't look at him. Mickey knew all about not having anyone. He would do what he could.

The door opened before Mickey knocked. Tracker stood on the other side, smiling. He had nice blue eyes and dark hair. The guy was honestly someone he could see as a news anchor or some shit. He was so polished.

"Damn. Do you ever leave those cameras?"

Tracker laughed. "I have an app on my phone that alerts me when the perimeter is breached. Then I can check the cameras from my phone."

Mickey nodded. That made sense.

Tracker waved him inside. "Come on."

Mickey stepped through the door and waited. He didn't want to leave the foyer and invade the guy's house. Tracker shut the door and headed for the sitting room. Mickey followed. They turned left and ended up in some den-like area. There was a table for presents and cake plus beer on ice. Mickey dropped his present on the table with the rest before inspecting the room. A few couches lined the walls. The way they didn't match made him wonder if they had been carried into the room for the party. He didn't recognize a few faces, but he knew there were brothers he hadn't met. They were down to only floor seating.

A smile exploded across Field's face when he spotted Mickey. "Mickey! Hey. You came."

Mickey returned his smile. "I said I would."

Field laughed. "I know, but I put you on the spot."

Mickey made a dismissive gesture. "Nah. I'm glad you asked. I wanted to come."

Field's smile made the claim worthwhile. He began pointing at people. "I know you know Tracker, of course, Edge, and Shadow and Rain. Obviously, you know Austen. You've met Ridge, Shore, and Scout briefly. But I don't know if you know Foster, Tidy, and Crisp."

Mickey shook their hands.

Crisp smiled the brightest. "Sorry we keep missing each other. Foster, Tidy, and I show up after the fun. Our planning sessions are usually separate."

Mickey shrugged. "It's cool. I figured we'd cross paths eventually."

Ice-blue eyes focused on him. "People don't cross paths with us unless they're dead."

Well, Foster seemed fun.

"All right." He didn't know what the guy expected him to say.

"Come have a seat." Edge stood, offering his spot. "Tracker was just getting ready to hand out the presents."

Mickey waved for him to sit. "I'm good on the floor." He dropped down to the empty spot in front of Edge and scooted back between his knees when Edge sat.

Edge immediately sat forward and set his hands on Mickey's shoulders. He spoke closely to Mickey's ear. "How was the rest of your day?"

Mickey answered quietly so he wouldn't interrupt the party and take focus away from the birthday boy. "Pretty boring. With Kylo down, I don't have shit to do."

Rain leaned his way, obviously over-hearing. "He's fine. Beau just feels guilty for neglecting him. He's been pampering him."

A smile exploded across Mickey's face. "Good. Kylo needs that."

"Wow! Someone has been talking to Austen." Field held up the jar of peanut butter Mickey had brought him.

Mickey laughed.

Edge obviously didn't think it was funny. "Damn. You drove two towns over and risked anaphylactic shock to get the organic peanut butter he likes? You're lucky you're not dead."

Mickey realized Edge had started out intending to keep the words between them. By the end, his voice had risen to where he had everyone's attention, especially Field's.

"You're allergic to peanuts?"

Mickey nodded. "It's fine. Don't worry about it."

Field hugged the jar to his chest. "You're allergic to peanut butter and risked death for me?"

An uncomfortable laugh escaped Mickey. "It wasn't quite that dramatic. Austen told me that's your favorite brand, so I sent a guy from work to pick it up. Likely, I would drop dead if I stepped one foot in that place, but I didn't go. Fabrice did. Then he gift-wrapped it for me just to be safe. So I was never in any real danger."

Field set the jar aside and stood. He crossed the room and dropped to his knees. "This would be a marriage proposal right now if I didn't have to give up peanuts for you."

Another uncomfortable laugh rumbled from him as Field's massive arms engulfed him. Seriously, the guy was huge. He could probably bench twice his weight, and that said a lot. Field was likely six-six and three twenty-five of solid muscle. It was just easy to forget how big he was with his golden retriever personality.

Mickey awkwardly patted Field's back. "I'm glad you like the gift."

Field pulled away and jumped to his feet. "Okay. Santa time."

Mickey looked around, confused. It was nowhere near Christmas. Sometimes Field said things that baffled him, except someone passed Field a Santa hat and he eagerly donned it. He wore a huge grin as he grabbed a badly wrapped present from a stack Mickey hadn't noticed.

"Shadow first."

Shadow did a happy clap before give-me hands like a little kid as Field passed him a present. He tore into it. Mickey didn't get to see what it was since a white box was shoved toward him.

"For you. It's not wrapped because I picked it up last minute."

Mickey reluctantly reached for it. "Thank you." Even Mickey heard the question in his voice.

"You're very welcome." For a heartbeat, right before Field turned away, Mickey caught a glimpse behind Field's mask. It froze his blood.

Luckily, Edge spoke against his ear, saving him. "Field doesn't believe in receiving gifts without reciprocation. This is really important for his mental health. Please go along."

Mickey pasted on a bright smile he didn't feel and lifted the lid on the box. It was a t-shirt with Edge's face printed on it. A surprised bark of laughter escaped him. Several people flashed proud smiles his way, as if praising him for being a good sport.

"Ah man. Your gift spoiled mine."

Mickey looked behind him at the comment. Edge held up a shirt with Mickey's picture on it. He couldn't stop laughing. "Oh my god. Where did you even get that picture?"

Field's smile was unrepentant. "Tracker pulled it off one of the recordings. I got your good side."

"My every side is good."

Everyone roared with laughter.

Edge leaned forward. "Damn right." He swiped his lips across Mickey's and Mickey's chest warmed. Edge wasn't hiding this... whatever it was. Mickey didn't know what to think, but he knew how he felt. Every moment with Edge felt good. He could get addicted to this.

He was a good person. Like, genuinely. Mickey had a good heart. He had no idea the story behind how Mickey ended up working for someone like Beau Bosi, but damn. He was wonderful.

Peanut butter was such a small thing to almost everyone. But not only was it something Field loved, Mickey had gotten him that gift at his own detriment. Then he had gone on to act like Field's gift brought him joy. Not just anyone would have stepped into that party and handled everything so beautifully. Edge couldn't get past it. By the end of the gathering, Mickey wore the shirt. Seeing Field's happiness was priceless to him. Mickey couldn't possibly know.

The moment they were in his bedroom alone, Edge had him hauled against him. His tongue was in Mickey's mouth, and he couldn't get enough. Mickey didn't question his intensity. He was right there, matching Edge's passion. Edge went straight for the button on Mickey's jeans, and they still stood a foot behind his closed door. The hunger he felt went way beyond physical. Mickey made him desperate for something bigger. He terrified Edge in a good way. Edge had thought of nothing else all day. He wanted to say it, but he couldn't think of a way to express himself without scaring him away. So he released the madness the only way he could. He ripped open the front of Mickey's jeans like a rabid fiend.

In a flash, he was over Mickey's shoulder and headed for the bed. No one had ever manhandled him like this. Edge loved it. Mickey tossed him onto the bed and covered Edge's body with his. He was everywhere.

"Am I allowed to do to you what you did to me last night?"

God. He was adorable. "You can do anything you want to me." He might have stopped to think a little harder about that one if he wasn't so horny. Mickey made him lose himself. That was a good thing. Edge did a decent job of hiding it, but he was ugly inside. One day, Mickey would see it and then never look back. Until that day, yeah. They would do whatever he wanted, and he would pray his mind didn't come unglued.

"Good." Mickey slithered down his body and had Edge's dick in his mouth before Edge had time to realize this was what he meant. Relief poured through him every bit as deeply as the pleasure of Mickey's hot mouth. Truthfully, it was obvious this was something Mickey didn't really do. Edge had never been more unbothered and happy. He was just overjoyed to have Mickey's mouth on him and his sanity mostly intact.

Edge tried to focus on everything Mickey did. He couldn't take it. Last night had been too amazing. He had to get inside Mickey again.

He pushed, urging Mickey onto his back. "Sorry. I just need to be inside you. You're too much temptation."

Mickey didn't look bothered. In fact, he looked turned on and ready to do anything.

Edge didn't do all the talking him through things again. This time, he worked quicker and pushed his way inside before he should. Mickey's entire body language screamed Edge had hurt him, but he didn't make a sound. If he protested, Edge wouldn't know because his brain short-circuited.

Edge scrambled away. "Sorry. I'm sorry. I didn't mean to—" He tried taking a few breaths. It didn't help. His vision darkened around the edges. Babbled words fell from his lips. He had a bad feeling he confessed things he never would. Edge wasn't sure Mickey heard a word either from trying to calm him.

"Take a breath. I'm fine. I swear I'm fine. You don't have to worry about me. Okay? I'd never agree to anything I couldn't handle. Just breathe."

Edge tried, but nothing happened.

Mickey climbed from the bed and yanked on his pants.

Fear of him leaving made everything twice as bad. "Please don't go. I'm sorry I'm a mess, but fuck. Don't go."

Mickey climbed back on to the bed and dragged Edge beneath him. He held him so tightly, he could barely draw the breath Mickey demanded he take. "I'm not going anywhere. You just need me dressed. I need you to know I'm not here for the sex. Please, just let me hold you while you do whatever this is."

The statement cut straight through his PTSD attack. His entire body shook with laughter. He practically felt the way Mickey had wanted to tell him to calm down, but didn't want to use those words. Edge swore he heard all the things Mickey was scared to say. He was a huge mess. There was no tiptoeing around that. When the laughter died, the embarrassment struck. Damn. All that had really happened. He wouldn't hear from Mickey again, and he completely understood. Edge wouldn't choose himself either.

"Well, shit. I really know how to ruin a good thing."

He felt Mickey smile against his ear. "Nothing is ruined. Do you want to hear something sad?"

Edge chuckled. "You have something humiliating you'd like to add? Please go ahead."

"This is the happiest I've ever been." He heard the sadness in Mickey's tone and felt it in his heart. Mickey didn't stop there. "I don't mean like it's sad because you just flipped out. It's because I'm holding you and it's the most I've ever been held in my life. I'm kind of scared it'll stop."

It hit Edge. Mickey's life was completely empty. He wasn't an employee. Not really. He didn't have the option to leave Beau. There was only one way someone in Mickey's position left their job and that involved a body bag. Beau wouldn't risk his family's safety by letting someone who had seen as much as Mickey go. So, who held Mickey? No one. God, Edge felt that.

He wrapped his arms around Mickey. "Would it be okay if we just stayed like this for a little while?"

"I don't want to disappoint you." Mickey sounded so sad.

Edge understood. Most men were like that. He might as well continue down the path of total humiliation to fix it. "Before last night, I hadn't had sex in years. You don't have to worry about disappointing me. I gave up a long time ago." Damn. Now he was the one who was sad.

Mickey touched his chin, turning Edge's face his way. He captured Edge's mouth in the sweetest kiss that lingered. Something beautiful blossomed between them. Edge didn't feel so much like he wanted to die. That was on Mickey.

Chapter Six

EDGE: *WILL I SEE you tonight?*

Mickey: *Yeah. It might be a little later than usual. Kylo wants a pajama party. Don't worry, though. Beau won't let him stay up too late.*

Edge: *I'll be here whenever you're free.*

Mickey: *Have you finished training for the night?*

Edge: *Just leaving. Want to sneak me in so we can fool around?*

Mickey: *Sounds amazing.*

Edge: *I got the flowers you sent. Field hasn't stopped teasing me yet.*

Mickey: *Oh no. I didn't consider that. Don't worry. I won't do it again. I just miss you.*

Edge: *No. I love them. Thank you. Field doesn't need an excuse to be ridiculous. Don't stop being you.*

Edge: *Also, I miss you too. See you tonight.*

The two months they spent meticulously planning this operation had been too long for Henry's blood. He knew they had to wait until both the buyer and the seller were in the same place at the same time. Plus, the boys had needed to practice to perfection. But that was the thing. There was too much to the tee about everything. Real life didn't work that way. How had these guys lived this long without detection? Surely, these plans didn't always go the way they did in the virtual world. If anything went wrong, they might have a war on their front lawn in a few hours, and then what? Henry would be forced to kill a lot of people. That was whatever. He didn't care about that, but innocent people lived in this house. They could get hurt.

The guys set up in Beau's personal sitting room. As they geared up, Henry paced. His temper frayed along with his nerves. "What is the deal with the LED masks? That seems kind of juvenile."

The look Tracker gave him proved he had insulted him. Tracker held up one of the masks and turned it to face Henry. "Not only does it have night vision and let me see everything everyone else does, but the guys can also swap views and see through each other's eyes."

"Plus, they really freak people out when they see death coming." Field laughed as he held up his own mask, which Henry had to admit was a bit more psychedelic compared to the rest.

Field set the mask aside. "You sure you don't want to come with, Daddy? I could keep you warm."

Henry rolled his eyes and went back to pacing. Tracker set up several monitors so they could watch from here, seeing everything the team saw. Admittedly, he kind of wanted to go with them, but not for the reasons Field suggested. The kid was relentless.

Henry turned and caught Edge eyeing Mickey in a way that made his blood boil. It wasn't the first time, and Henry was just irritated enough to say something. He kept his voice low, though, so he wouldn't embarrass Mickey.

"Don't look at him like that. Even if Mickey wasn't straight, he'd never touch murderous trash like this crew."

Edge's eyebrows shot up. "I'm not sure what to address first. Trash? This murderous trash is about to save everyone in this house's ass. Straight? Wouldn't touch me? Maybe you should tell Mickey that, since we've been fucking for months."

The red haze that coated his vision scared even him. Edge had spoken every word so calmly, Henry couldn't call him a liar. He looked Mickey's way. Mickey laughed as he tried to pull the hood of Field's jacket over his head—like they were friends... who saw each other all the time.

The distance disappeared between them. Henry had Mickey by the arm, dragging him into the next room before he knew what he would do. He slammed the door shut before pushing Mickey against the wall.

"What the hell, Henry?"

"Tell me it's not true."

A deep line appeared between Mickey's eyebrows. "What's not true?"

"That you're fucking Edge."

Mickey's expression snapped closed. "Oh."

Fuck. It was true. There was an invisible knife sticking in his heart and twisting. "You're supposed to be straight. You have to be because, otherwise—" He motioned between them, incapable of finding the words for how he felt.

"I don't—" Mickey looked every bit as confused as he should.

Henry tried again. "How can you not know? It's always been." He motioned between them again. Henry didn't have words. He didn't talk about feelings. But the fucking betrayal, he fucking felt that shit. "You're supposed to be straight."

"Oh." Mickey looked shell-shocked. His entire demeanor shifted. The pity made him sick.

Henry couldn't take it. He opened the door and shoved Mickey back into the sitting room with the same level of violence he had pulled him away. Mickey stumbled from the force. Without a plan but to make the pain and humiliation stop, Henry grabbed Field and yanked him into the room, slamming the door again. They were eye to eye.

"Abuse me, Daddy." He had pretty green eyes... just like Mickey. They danced with laughter, exactly the way Mickey's always did.

"You really think you can handle me?" He shoved Field to his knees. "Prove it."

"Yes, sir."

Henry stared at the wall and ignored the humor in Field's voice that obviously couldn't be muted. Even as he hardened on Field's talented tongue, he felt nothing. He saw nothing. Not even the expensive wallpaper right in front of him. Years he had spent hopelessly loving Mickey rose to the surface to choke him. He had been okay with Mickey being straight. That was something he couldn't change standing in their way. That meant he never had to admit anything. He could just feel what he felt without losing a thing. Now, he knew the truth and he couldn't deal. Everything he wanted was gone. What did that leave him?

Edge couldn't unsee Henry's face or the way Mickey had looked as Henry shoved him out of that room. The pains in his chest wouldn't quit. He had to keep his head in the game. Henry's expression wouldn't budge. He had seen that look before. Edge couldn't get warm. His blood was like ice. A weight sat on his chest. He had been here before.

Edge sat alone on the rooftop and stared through his scope. By rote, he went through the motions. His body was on autopilot, saved by his training, while his mind left him. It had to go away. His sanity couldn't survive this again. That jealous hatred. The ugly things it did. He couldn't.

"Let's get started." Tracker's voice cut through the mic. Edge watched Rain and Shadow move through the building like they were invisible. He watched them pause right before reaching their targets and settle themselves.

"Go now."

Edge saw the blood spatter and heard the useless gunfire. Nothing penetrated the ghosts haunting him. Not even the beauty of the way they had devised to leave no trace of themselves.

"Building clear. Mission complete."

Edge swept the area once more through his scope and broke down his weapon. Another job. More money. It meant nothing. This reason he gave himself to exist was just that—a meaningless way to extend a pointless life. He had honestly thought he had found something with Mickey. That was just like him, though. He should have known.

"Cleaning crew headed in for a quick check for trace evidence. The van is waiting. Get a move on, guys."

Edge put his equipment away and slung his bag over his shoulders before quickly making his way back to the ground. Just as they planned it, the entire team reunited outside and climbed inside the waiting van. The smell of blood permeated the air, adding to the horrible memories trying to choke him.

"Are you okay?"

At Rain's quietly spoken question, he looked around. Everyone stared at him.

Edge cleared his throat. "Yeah. Proof of payment, Tracker."

"Yep. Payment complete. Funds came through before the last body even hit the floor. It seems Beau was happy with the service."

Edge smiled, but he didn't feel it. He didn't feel anything but the cold fingers of the past wrapped around his throat, choking him.

"That's great. Hopefully, this will lead to more jobs in the future. This could be a lucrative client for us." Edge tried like hell to keep up pretenses. His gaze met Field's and his efforts died. Those green eyes saw everything. They saw right through him. Edge didn't think he would last much longer.

Beau was all smiles. He couldn't stop saying how impressed he was with the show. He wasn't wrong. As sickening as it had been to watch, the operation had also kept Mickey totally transfixed. It had been so perfectly orchestrated—like watching art unfold. Still, Mickey felt so fucking sick, he didn't know where to look or what to do. He felt the coldness of Henry's stare. No texts came from Edge. Everything felt wrong. Edge hadn't even looked at him before he left. He had no clue what had transpired between Henry and him to upend his life like this. It wasn't like he could ask Henry, and Edge wouldn't respond to his texts.

"I'm headed to bed. Go, enjoy your nights. You two deserve to relax after all this looking over our shoulders lately."

Henry slapped Beau's shoulder at the order and strolled from the room with him. Mickey seized his chance. He didn't look back. In a flash, he was out the door and backing out of the garage. He couldn't stay and face another conversation with Henry. Everything felt wrong. When had Henry... what was he even thinking? Henry had been so furious, but he hadn't actually explained a thing. All Mickey's interpretations were suffocating him. His fears were doing even more damage. Henry had kept saying Mickey was supposed to be straight. Had he said that to Edge? Was that why he wouldn't talk to Mickey? Maybe this all circled back to the night he thought he had hurt Mickey. Fuck. He didn't know.

At Edge's place, he had to stop himself from running for the door. He didn't even know if they were back yet. Tracker opened the front door before he reached it, the way he always did.

"Hey, man. Edge is in his room. Feel free to head that way."

Mickey flashed a smile he didn't feel. "Thanks. You did great tonight." He didn't wait to see how what felt like an odd compliment landed. Mickey had to get to Edge. When he let himself in, it was every bit as bad as he feared.

Dead eyes met his stare.

Mickey swallowed past the lump in his throat. "Hey. You didn't answer my texts."

"Most people get the hint from that."

Ouch. Goddamn. "Okay. Most people have the balls to say why." Mickey didn't even bother shutting the door. He wouldn't be here long, it seemed.

A long, obviously tired sigh slipped from Edge. "Look. I've done the whole falling in love before with someone who already has someone powerful in love with them. It never ends well for me. While I'm not sure if Henry is quite that violent and I'm not at the disadvantage I once was, I still won't do this again. So, it's been real."

"It's been real." Mickey repeated the words, letting them fill his veins with ice. "That's all you've got?"

"I thought that's all you expected. You wanted to be told. You've been told."

Mickey wouldn't beg or let Edge see him hurt. A smirk pulled at his lips. He couldn't believe this was happening. "Funny. It doesn't seem like it's been real at all." He walked away without looking back. No one tried to stop him, even though he saw their faces. They had heard every word. Mickey swore he would never forget how he felt at that moment. He would never put himself in the position to feel this way again.

He climbed into his SUV. The passenger side door opened, and Field hopped into the passenger seat. Mickey froze and simply stared at him.

Field didn't look his way. "Just drive, okay?"

There was something in his voice. Mickey did as told. He drove away with no real destination in mind. While he didn't know what Field wanted, he was glad for the excuse to not go home.

"We were raised in a Russian spy program. All of us," Field added, unnecessarily.

Mickey held his tongue and just listened.

"In Russia, couples are paid to have children. It's some family values bullshit, but anyhow. They're paid more for their second child. Nearly double. A lot of couples don't want a second child. They just want the money so they can buy their apartments or whatever. That didn't start until the early two thousands, but what most people don't know is, it's been secretly happening forever. Under the table, the government struck deals with willing couples. Allow the woman to carry a very genetically engineered fetus to term. For all the trouble, the couple gets a payout of around fifty grand. It's a very lucrative deal for most people. Don't get me wrong. There are risks involved when it comes to making the perfect baby. But the men, they are willing to sacrifice."

That sounded awful, but Mickey's jaw didn't move. Very little shocked him.

"Those of us who were created to be the perfect soldier, we were raised together. We trained together. Groups were formed, matching perfect skills. Being gay, that's unacceptable, but still, we found each other."

Field took a breath. "Rain is very beautiful, is he not?"

It struck Mickey how Russian Field sounded tonight and how much he hid. "I mean, yeah, I suppose." Honestly. Mickey had only noticed in a passing sort of way. Apparently, he needed to be abducted to really want someone.

"He is beautiful to his detriment," Field said, sounding as if he saw something in his head that distracted him. "He caught many eyes during training. It didn't matter he was much too young. He possessed something alluring that called to people—even those who had no desire to be gay. In fact, had a special hatred for it. But most of all, Edge was intoxicated."

The desire to puke doubled. He didn't want to know this. Everything felt like it was crushing him.

Field wouldn't stop. "There was a commander. He came to Rain in the night, hiding his sickness in the dark. He was obsessed. Dangerously so. That didn't stop Rain and Edge from getting closer. When the commander learned of their relationship, he had Edge taken to be made an example of what happened to those who dared to participate in unnatural activities. He was tortured in ways you can't imagine." Field stared at nothing. His voice turned absent. "I wish I could not imagine too."

Mickey rubbed his chest. He heard the demons Field kept hidden.

They didn't stop Field from spilling their secrets. "You see, I saw the moment Edge realized Henry loves you. I saw his eyes. He returned to the past and didn't come back."

Mickey still didn't know what Field wanted to hear. He hadn't done anything to deserve any of this. None of them had, but goddamn it. Edge had decided for them, and there was nothing he could do. He was so fucking pissed; he didn't know if he would if he could.

Thankfully, Field obviously didn't expect anything from Mickey. "You can drop me off here. I can find my way home. I just wanted you to know it's not you. You're a good person. You just found yourself in the middle of a group of completely fucked up people. I get that you didn't ask for any of this. But thanks for taking a chance on us. Most people wouldn't."

Mickey deflated. "I'm not leaving you on the side of the road, for fuck's sake. I'm upset, but I'm not an asshole. Plus, I really do like you. I haven't been just putting up with you guys to be with Edge. You're my friends. Well, I'm yours. I can't make anyone feel the same about me... obviously. But I care and I'm not going anywhere, okay? We're still good."

Field didn't respond. When he did, he still sounded lost in his head. "I don't want to go home. Do you want to go home?"

Mickey didn't need to think about it. "No." There was nothing for him at home but awkward silence and anger. He didn't care if he ever made it home again.

Chapter Seven

HENRY WASN'T THE LEAST bit surprised when Mickey didn't show up for his shift. He might have panicked if he didn't keep track of Mickey's phone. Beau never knew anyone's schedule and had been all about Kylo the entire morning, so he didn't notice. He didn't have to go far to find him. Mickey was slumped over the steering wheel of his SUV, completely out. Field was in the passenger seat, every bit as dead to the world. Henry opened the door and beer cans and liquor bottles fell out. He pinched the spot between his eyes.

"Dumbass." He didn't doubt for a second Mickey had driven like this. Mickey had never given a shit about himself. It made him irresistible to people just like him because, while he didn't care about himself, he deeply cared about everyone else.

With a sigh, he lifted Mickey from the vehicle and carried him inside. It took him a minute to avoid everyone in the house to get to Mickey's bedroom unseen. When he dumped Mickey on the bed, he didn't budge. Henry checked his breathing. He was alive but knocked all the way out.

Henry backtracked and got Field. He got to Mickey's bedroom quicker this time since he had already found the empty path. He dropped Field on the bed and went to work. Once he had their shoes off, he tucked Mickey under the covers first. Even drunk, he was beautiful. He wouldn't be creepy and stare. Henry did that enough every day. He already felt like an ass. Henry moved to Field's side of the bed and got him under the covers. Then he couldn't move. Field looked like a totally different person asleep. It was like unhappiness etched his every line. Henry sat on the edge of the bed. Every second that passed, the worse he felt. He was a bad person. Of course he was. He had sold his soul decades ago in Italy. Henry had a best friend with more talent at making deals than either of them had morals. Henry would do anything to protect Beau, and he had over the years. People didn't get to the top with clean hands. Still, Mickey and Field hadn't deserved to be dropped in his path. Yet here they were.

He swiped his fingers through Field's hair. Henry still couldn't believe the guy hadn't balked even a second before dropping to his knees. "You really are a fucked-up mess, huh?"

"I'm sorry."

Henry's gaze shot to Mickey's side of the bed. His voice sounded like shit, but he was awake. "Why? You better be about to say for drinking and driving."

Mickey didn't react to the humor in his voice. He didn't say anything. Mickey just held his stare, looking half out of his head.

Henry circled the bed again and sat on the edge at Mickey's side. He didn't know how lucid Mickey actually was, but Henry couldn't look away. He leaned sideways and braced his weight on the mattress, boxing Mickey in. It was as close as he would ever get to holding him. "I was upset last night, but I hope you know you can talk to me. Why are you sorry?"

Pain swam in Mickey's eyes. "You didn't say anything. All these years, you didn't say anything. Why? Maybe I wouldn't have fallen in love with an asshole who doesn't want me, if you had told me. I've always been closer to you than anyone else. Now I'll never know."

Henry had never hated himself more, and that was saying something. Mickey didn't deserve this. Henry had told himself a lot of things to stay away from Mickey because he had always known Mickey was too good for him. Now Mickey suffered because Henry was a bastard.

"Forget it, okay?" He kissed Mickey's forehead. The ache in his chest made him angry. He wasn't supposed to feel anything. When he pulled away, Mickey was out again. Henry had to walk away. As he made his way down the stairs, the doorbell rang like kids trying to get Halloween candy. Henry cursed under his breath as he rushed to answer. He had a bad feeling he knew who was on the other side. Henry didn't have the patience for this today. He jogged the last few steps when the ringing got out of control.

Henry yanked open the door. "This is a fucking home. A family lives here. God-damn. It couldn't be more obvious no one taught any of you any manners."

The entire Agafonov crew stood on the stoop, looking various states of terrified. "Give us our Field."

Their reactions and Shadow's demand proved Henry was right to think Field was a loose cannon. Still. He was angry with the world today, especially with this crew. "If you can't keep up with your people, that's not my problem."

The pretty boy, Tracker, visibly got his hackles up. "I always know where everyone is at all times. We know Field is here."

"He's with Mickey. Upstairs. Second to the last door on the left."

Henry spun at Kylo's drive-by info. "How in the fuck?"

Kylo giggled and kept going. He dragged a mesh bag of stuffed animals behind him, heading for the living room.

Before he could say a word, he totally lost control. Combat boots stormed up the stairs. Edge brought up the rear. Their gazes met. Henry stepped in his path. His rage kept him from being silent. No one hurt Mickey.

The fury in Henry's expression was exactly what Edge expected. Today, he was a little better prepared for it. Last night had been the second type of PTSD attack Edge suffered. It was the one that

Mickey hadn't seen yet. He had a clearer mind today. Edge had back his usual icy calm. There was nothing Henry could do to him.

"Say what you have to say."

Henry ran his tongue over his teeth. It was obvious he bit back all the words. He definitely wanted to hit Edge. Edge watched him take a calming breath, proving his love wasn't toxic. "There's nothing I can think of to say that's bad enough for knowing he loves you. *You.* The piece of shit who doesn't even want him. There is no description for how badly I want to break you. But unlike you, I do love him. If hurting you pains him even in the slightest, I can't do it. With that said, I'm not going anywhere. The second I know he's over you, you'll see me again."

"Noted." Edge stepped around Henry and followed his brothers up the stairs. He found them trying to wake Field, who was in bed with Mickey. The smell of alcohol permeated the air.

While everyone else tried waking Field or hovering like worried hens, Edge moved to Mickey's side of the bed. Even though, in his heart, Edge knew Field would never hurt him by sleeping with Mickey, he was still relieved to see they were both fully dressed.

He massaged Mickey's arms. "Hey, baby. You still alive?"

Mickey didn't react.

Edge got worried he really might be dead. He checked his pulse. It was strong. Still, he dug his phone out, ready to call nine-one-one.

Shadow jumped in. "Oh, for fuck's sake." He twisted Field's nipple—hard.

Field shot up like a bolt. "What? Holy shit! What's wrong?" He looked around. "Oh." He snuggled back down and pulled the covers high. "Go away and let me sleep."

Shadow smacked his thigh. "We thought you might be dead in a ditch somewhere. You scared us."

Field didn't bother opening his eyes again. "Bullshit. Tracker always knows where we are." He snagged Mickey around the waist and pulled him close like a teddy bear. "Just because none of you want to keep Mickey doesn't mean I don't. Go be pricks somewhere else."

Edge really wanted to blow up, but he knew that wasn't the right thing to do after last night. He had to stay calm. He rubbed Field's arm. "I appreciate you staying with him, but he's not waking up, Field. He might need medical attention."

Field's head lifted. He stared down at Mickey, inspecting him. Field licked his face from chin to forehead.

Mickey came awake like he was ready to throw hands. "What the fuck?"

Field went back to snuggling beneath the covers. "See? He's good."

Mickey blinked at the crowd surrounding the bed. "Why wouldn't I be good?" He immediately heaved. "Wait. I'm not good." Mickey scrambled from the bed and into the nearby bathroom.

Edge followed. He stood by, ready to jump in and do whatever was needed.

This was definitely a case of better out than in. An arm appeared in the doorway, holding a Gatorade. Edge had no idea where it came from, but he accepted it.

Finally, Mickey collapsed against the wall. He truly looked like hell. His gaze slid toward Edge. He definitely didn't look happy to see him. "Why are you here?"

Yeah. He definitely wasn't thrilled. "For you." He passed the drink to Mickey. "I said a lot of shit last night that I didn't mean. The whole thing with Henry triggered me in a bad way. My history, it's—"

"Bad," Mickey said, interrupting him like he couldn't listen to another word. "Yeah. I gathered as much. Do you know what? So is mine. I was homeless nearly my entire life. Do you know what happens to homeless kids on the street? Go on, guess." Thankfully, he didn't get to say a word. Mickey was obviously too furious. "I'm sure you'll have no trouble figuring it out. But do you know what? I'm not currently sitting here, trying to destroy you with my bullshit. Not once have I used my trauma as a crutch or a weapon against you. I get it, okay. You don't want this. It's fine. You can go."

Edge rubbed his forehead. "That's the thing I'm trying to say. I don't want to go. You're what I want. I just don't know, okay? I never meant to hurt you."

"Yes, you did." Mickey held his stare. Despite obviously being half dead, he didn't sound any less certain of his mind. "Every word you said was meant to hit its mark—me. You can have all the excuses, and they can be good ones, but that still doesn't mean I have to let you treat me like shit to soothe yourself. I deserve better. I deserve someone who loves me back."

Edge flinched. Henry had claimed Mickey loved him, but he hadn't believed. He thought the words were meant to strike at him. But now Mickey basically confirmed his claim, and Edge had really fucked up because Mickey was right. Edge had intentionally hurt him, and Mickey had done nothing but treat him like a king. He didn't deserve to be treated the way Edge treated him, and no excuse was good enough to expect Mickey's forgiveness. That was something earned.

"You're right. I can't be sorry enough to excuse the way I hurt you."

Mickey fought his way off the floor. "Good. Now that you know what everyone else already knew, I'm going to go cuddle up with Field, pass out, and pray for death. Have a nice life."

Edge stepped into his path. "Please, Mickey. I know how much more amazing you were to me than I ever was to you. You gave me pieces of yourself you've never given anyone and I know it. Please give me a chance to make things right."

Mickey stared at him in silence, and Edge saw the truth. He had killed something beautiful inside Mickey. Henry had thought Mickey was straight for a reason—because Mickey had thought it too. Then Edge had blown his life to pieces. He didn't deserve a second chance.

Edge stepped out of the way. "Be careful with Field. He has terrifying nightmares that make him dangerous."

"I'm not worried." He headed for the bed. "Maybe he'll do me a solid and kill me." Mickey sat his drink on the bedside table and fell into bed. Field immediately had him back in his arms, holding him the way Edge used to do. The entire crew still stood there, witnessing the next downfall of his life. He really wished—just once—they didn't see him at his lowest.

Edge motioned for the door. "Let's go. He'll be fine here."

They filed out. No one met his stare. Thankfully, he didn't cross Henry's path again. Maybe he would let the guy put him out of his misery. Then they could both be happy.

Chapter Eight

MICKEY FELT LIKE DEATH, but he couldn't miss a second day of work. The life had gone from him, and he couldn't fake it. This wasn't a job he could quit, but he desperately wanted to walk away from everything. Henry never looked at him. Every breath hurt. The emptiness was back, and he drowned in it.

"You look so sad and you're not eating your cookies."

Mickey glanced down at his tiny saucer and teacup. He had always secretly loved these tea parties with Kylo. Mickey hadn't gotten a childhood. Being with

Kylo was as close as he would ever get to those stolen days. "Sorry. I'm still not one hundred percent."

Kylo's eyes flashed with kindness. "Daddy should've let you have the day off so you can fully recover. I don't want a repeat of what you went through last time."

The last time Mickey had gotten sick, the flu had completely taken him down. It had turned to pneumonia and continued to morph until he damn near ended up hospitalized. He'd lost forty pounds he had only recently started to regain. Now, the thought of putting food in his mouth made him want to heave.

"I've missed spending time with you. There's no reason for me to go back to bed. Plus, Beau isn't here. Do you really want to spend the day with someone else?" Mickey tried hard to give him a playful yet pitiful face, as if begging Kylo not to hurt his feelings.

Kylo set his hand on Mickey's arm. His light blue eyes saw too much. Kylo probably knew more than anyone else did simply because he was observant in ways no one else was.

"Did you know I lived with Rain for a while?"

Mickey rolled with the subject change. "I did not."

Kylo nodded. "We were in a year-long production together, doing eight shows a week. I lived alone, but we were always together. It seems that made me a target, completely unbeknownst to me, of course. One night, I was attacked in the parking lot after a show and Rain took everyone out before I could even blink, much less be scared. Afterward, he was obviously forced to explain a lot of things to me, and I moved in with him to stay safe. They have a very odd household." Kylo stared into space for a moment. "I miss them. Field always threw the best birthday Christmases. He gave me my first tea set." He blinked and looked down. "As a matter of fact, it was this one."

Mickey dropped his gaze to the table. He had always assumed Beau had bought the set. One thing Mickey had become an expert at since moving in with Beau was luxury. The tea set was worth a fortune.

They both looked up at the same time and their stares met. Mickey couldn't look away. Kylo lowered his voice as if anyone would overhear in the privacy of Kylo's playroom.

"He's terrifying, you know. Everyone sees the jokester, but it's not real. I think he scares himself."

That didn't surprise Mickey.

Kylo sat back, obviously moving on. "Anyhow, one thing I noticed there was Edge. He always fascinated me. No one treats him like a friend. It always made me a little sad. They follow him like he's proven he's stronger than them, but no one ever sat with him or seemed to fully include him. He lived on the outskirts of the group. Everyone else seemed to have someone who they were always paired with. Not Edge. He was always rigid and cold. But sometimes, I would catch the longing way he watched every-one else. I saw the way he fully recognized he was the outsider, but he didn't know how to break past that. Something stood in the way. I don't know what, though."

Mickey knew. Edge stood in his own way. He had been tortured for loving Rain. Edge kind of hated him for it and everyone knew it, but no one said it. Mickey had seen it but hadn't understood it until Field's confessions. The entire crew would never split, but Edge feared connections in a way the rest didn't. That didn't mean he didn't crave what he had lost. Edge just didn't know how to love anymore. Mickey couldn't be his punching bag while he figured it out.

Fabrice appeared in the doorway. "These came for you, Mickey." He held a huge bouquet of red roses.

Mickey's eyebrows shot to his hairline.

He accepted the flowers while Kylo squealed on his behalf. "Thank you." With his heart in his throat, Mickey opened the tiny card attached.

I wanted to claim these were from Field, so maybe you'd accept them, but I can't be that much of a coward. So, maybe still don't throw them in the trash. You deserve them.

—Edge

Mickey put the card back and kept his mind on lockdown.

"They're so pretty. Daddy got me flowers after the whole milk thing. They've been dead for a good while now, though. I just don't have the heart to throw them away."

"You can have these, if you want." Mickey wasn't sure if he meant it, but he still remembered exactly how Edge had looked at him as he kicked him from his life. He still felt every eye on him as he left that house. Every time he had put his pride on the line and let Edge use him in every way sat on his chest and kept him awake at night. He was more confused than he had ever been. Edge had made him feel things he never had. He couldn't risk himself again like that.

"No. Thank you, though. I can't take them. Red roses are very personal. They represent love. You can't pass that to someone else."

Mickey's gaze locked on Kylo at the claim. Affection rose in his chest, choking him. He had been in his feelings for so long without anyone noticing. He couldn't take it anymore. "I love you."

Kylo melted in a way only he could. He was so innocent in a way that couldn't be described. Kylo deserved the world and all the kindness.

"When you had that attack, I've never been that scared. I know I never say it, but you're really all I have. It would've killed me if anything had happened to you."

Kylo stood and circled the table. He wrapped his arms around Mickey and held on. "You saved my life that day. Only the fact that you knew exactly what was wrong and had the tools to fix it is what kept me alive. You have no idea how much I love you. You're like the closest person to me next to Beau. Don't tell Rain, okay?"

Mickey laughed. He hated how watery it sounded. He was dangerously close to tears.

Kylo moved back to his chair and wiped his eyes. "Eat your cookie."

Mickey laughed again and picked up the cookie. He felt a little better. His gaze moved to the flowers. Red meant love. It seemed he had maybe heard that somewhere.

Fabrice reappeared. "Sorry to continue to interrupt your teatime. This just arrived as well." He crossed the room and handed Mickey a wrapped box.

Mickey eyed the bright paper. "Thank you. You deserve a raise for the continuous stair climbing."

"Buns of steel," Fabrice said as he walked away.

Kylo and Mickey exchanged a glance before bursting into laughter. Fabrice always knew how to deliver a deadpan line. The chef was low-key hilarious.

"Open it." Kylo bounced in his seat. He looked more than a little excited to see the gift.

Mickey tugged the ribbon loose before tearing into the paper. He opened the flaps on the box and blinked at the contents. His throat swelled. The emotional roller coaster continued. He lifted out the LED mask. Each one was unique to each member of the crew. He inspected it, turning on the lights. His had blue lights.

"Oh, wow. Those things are crazy advanced and stupidly expensive and time consuming to make. It's like they made you part of the family. That's... wow."

Mickey pulled out the card inside and opened it.

You will always be one of us.

It was signed by all the guys.

Mickey's eyes filled with tears. He had to look away. Mickey didn't have a family. That was why it had cut him so deeply to leave behind Edge and his brothers. He had gotten so close to everyone, only to be shoved out the door.

Fabrice reappeared in the doorway.

"Oh, for fuck's sake. What now?" Mickey would cry if anything else happened.

Fabrice stepped aside. "You have a visitor."

Edge stood in the doorway, looking unsure of his welcome. He wore the t-shirt with Mickey's face on it. Gah. Mickey couldn't take it.

Kylo waved. "Hi, Edge. Love the t-shirt."

A sweet but unsure smile touched Edge's lips. "Thanks. Mickey has one similar to it. If he hasn't taken scissors to it yet, which would be totally fair."

"Why is everyone in here?"

Fabrice looked slightly horrified at getting caught by Beau outside the kitchen. It was worse since he stood inside Beau's bedroom, staring into Kylo's playroom. "*Excusez.*" He scrambled from the room.

Beau's gaze followed him. "He's the only one supposed to be in here, feeding Kylo."

Mickey hid a smile. His emotions were all over the place.

Kylo popped to his feet. "You're home."

Beau strolled into the room, leaving Edge behind in the doorway. His hand appeared from behind his back. He held roses. "I brought you flowers to replace the ones you refuse to let the staff throw away, but I see someone beat me to it."

"Don't be silly. Those are Mickey's." He skipped across the room and met Beau halfway. The happiness of just seeing each other was beautiful to watch, especially since they had only been apart for a few hours.

Before Beau could ask anything about Mickey, thankfully, Kylo was in his arms, distracting him.

Mickey's gaze slid Edge's way.

Edge waited patiently, obviously determined to stay.

Beau's gaze never wavered from Kylo. "You two should get lost. I won't need you again today, Mickey." He turned, holding Kylo's hand as if to head to their bedroom. His gaze locked on Edge's shirt. "Take tomorrow off, Mickey. You look like hell."

Edge stepped out of the way, letting the pair pass.

Mickey stood and gathered his things. "Come on. We'll head out through this other door and give them their privacy."

Edge nodded. He glanced around as he moved Mickey's way. "This is a gorgeous dance room. Has Rain seen this? Minus the playroom, he'd be jealous."

"Yeah. He's been in here." Mickey didn't look at Edge. He couldn't. Mickey carefully placed the mask in the box.

Edge grabbed the roses for him. "That mask is fully functional. It's an open invitation to join us for any mission."

"I appreciate the trust, but I'd only be in the way. Your team is better off without me." He walked toward the door that led into the hallway without looking to see if Edge followed.

Edge was right on his heels. "We're really not. I'm not."

Mickey didn't respond. He never knew what to say. Conversation was uncomfortable to him, especially the hard talks. He made his way to his bedroom so they could speak privately.

Edge closed the door behind him. "Where would you like these?" He motioned with the roses, showing what he meant.

Mickey glanced around, looking for a spot, and it hit him. He wanted the flowers. If they meant love, he wanted that too. "On the dresser, I suppose. It kind of gets sunlight. Do they need sunlight? I don't know shit about flowers."

Edge shrugged. "I don't know. Probably." He put them where Mickey had indicated. "They look good right here, though." While he worked to center the flowers in exactly the middle of the dresser, Edge spoke as if he couldn't do so while looking at Mickey. "I guess I could've brought these over myself since I was coming. But I know they made it safely this way, and I wasn't sure if I'd lose my nerve halfway here. This household isn't like mine. No one batted an eye at you getting flowers and Beau showed up with them too."

Mickey sat on the edge of the bed and watched Edge. "Love is a good thing here. It hasn't always lived under this roof. This was actually a pretty miserable job before Kylo came along." Actually, it had improved quite a bit after Beau's first wife committed suicide, but Mickey didn't want to say that. He might have done the same in her shoes.

When it became obvious Edge couldn't fuss with the flowers any longer, he paced. His gaze still steered clear of Mickey. "Are you okay? Have you fully recovered from your binge?"

"No."

"Oh. Can I get you something? Another Gatorade? Something for a headache?"

He truly was the guy who looked out for everyone else, all while knowing he would get zero love in return. "No. I mean, I'm not okay."

Edge stopped pacing and focused on him. "What's wrong?" He really looked concerned and totally convinced Mickey was over him. Just like that.

"I'm not okay because I'm in love with you and I know you'll never love me back. You care. I know that much, but I don't think love is something you'll ever give anyone."

Edge didn't react and still Mickey felt how deeply his words cut. "Maybe some people can't be deprogrammed." He made a helpless motion. "It's like I'm one of two people and I don't know how to be something in between. Either I'm the biggest mess anyone has ever seen, or I'm the one in control. Without that tight hold, then I'm always that first one. But the hardest thing about being the guy who holds it all together is that everyone sees me exactly the way you do. Do you really think I don't love my brothers? That I'm incapable. Do you honestly believe I don't love you?"

Mickey heard it weaved through his monotonous tone. The hurt. The bitterness. The love. But Mickey needed him to break past this with at least him or he would always be the one tossed in the street every time something triggered him.

"I don't know. There's a part of me that wants to believe, but I had believed with every fiber of my being that we were perfect, and I was wrong."

"I'm sorry."

"I don't want to hear that you're sorry."

Edge's mask slipped. "Then what do you want to hear? What do you need me to say? Because I don't know how to be who you want. But I love you and I'm trying my ass off here, whether you see it or not. I know you don't want to hear it, but I'm sorry I'm damaged. I'm devastated that I failed you. You're the only person who has ever come to that house just for me. I'm pretty sure you're the only person who even realizes I'm human and now you're saying you don't see me either."

Mickey didn't think Edge realized he cried or shouted. But Mickey saw the walls falling. He couldn't look away from the passion the real Edge showed.

He held Mickey's stare, looking completely wrecked. "I need you to... I just need you."

"Come here."

Edge looked defeated as he crossed the room.

Mickey snagged Edge's hips and towed him closer until he stood between Mickey's knees. He didn't release him. "When you were breaking things off, tell me what was going through your head."

Edge's hands rose and fell. "I don't know. It was just like my brain was trapped in a loop of fear and anger. No logic whatsoever cut through. It was like I stood by helpless, watching myself wreck everything, and I couldn't stop it. But you've already told me you don't want to hear excuses."

Mickey massaged Edge's hips. "I'm asking for a reason because I need to know what your plan is to stop it in the future.

If you can't tell me you're trying, then why should I?"

"I talked to Austen. He started me on some meds. It's too soon to know if they'll work, but if they don't, he says there're others we can try."

Try was exactly the word he wanted to hear. There was no hope for them if nothing changed. "Okay. Do you love me?"

Edge's features softened. He set his hands on Mickey's shoulders—like he wanted to touch Mickey but was scared of rejection. "I do. If you need me to say it in some certain tone, then I'm doomed to fail you. All I can do is say I love you and keep saying it until you—hopefully—believe."

Mickey urged him even closer. "I hope you intend to keep saying it. Otherwise, it'll be a long life for me without affirmation. Plus, I intend to say it—a lot. I love you. Not the guy who leads successful missions, even though I know that's you. I love you. The human behind all of that. That's the guy I love. Can I please fucking have him? Because I thought we were happy."

"It hurts me to hear you ask for my love when you don't deserve to have to do that. I hate that I destroyed something so amazing. Fuck."

Mickey felt his frustration. He shot to his feet and claimed Edge's mouth. The ugly desperation he had felt the past few days poured into their kiss. He didn't want to be alone again.

Edge always felt so much that it choked him and made him useless in any sort of relationship. People thought he was cold. Really, he just didn't know how to be like everyone else. From the very beginning, it was like Mickey saw him. Edge didn't know how to lose him. He didn't think he could survive it. Edge was equally aware he didn't deserve forgiveness.

Mickey chuckled against his lips. "I can't believe you wore this shirt."

Edge had no shame any longer. "I ran errands in it too."

Mickey laughed harder.

"You should put yours on and we could go to lunch."

Mickey's sexy green gaze held his stare. "Or you could take yours off and stay here."

"I can do that."

Mickey slowly pushed the shirt up Edge's torso while he held Edge's stare. Edge couldn't look away. Just like the very first time he saw those eyes in his rearview mirror, he was transfixed. Bewitched.

"I don't know what happened to me the first time I saw you, but I've never felt so obsessed." He thought he would feel embarrassed or dumb talking about his feelings, but he didn't. "You were in the back of that van, and I looked up and caught your gaze in the mirror. Something about you just struck me." Mickey removed Edge's shirt and Edge kept spilling his every thought, even as Mickey unbuttoned his jeans. "You were so cocky and sure I would regret ever fucking with you. I don't know. You just made me crave... life, I guess. I wanted." Edge paused. He didn't want to sound pitiful, but he was. "I wanted you to see me too."

Mickey slowly slid the zipper down on Edge's jeans. His gaze never wavered from holding Edge's stare. "I see you."

He knew that. "Please don't stop."

"You should make love to me."

At Mickey's statement, Edge worked his shirt up and over his head, revealing Mickey's sexy upper body. It was so obvious how hard he worked on his body, and Edge loved it. The guy was ten years older than Edge and looked way better. He knew Mickey had to stay in shape so he could protect Kylo, and Edge loved looking at him, but Edge also knew he would love Mickey no matter how he looked. That didn't stop him from lowering his head and licking the nipple that had his attention.

Mickey moaned.

Edge's entire body reacted to the sound from his mind to his toes. Mickey got him hotter than anyone ever had. He went to work on Mickey's jeans, unbuttoning and unzipping them before pushing them down his hips. Edge just wanted to be closer. He wanted to feel his skin against him.

They pushed and tugged at each other's clothes until they were nude. Mickey kept capturing Edge's mouth like he couldn't stop. Their kisses were always so intense, Edge had no idea how they ended up on the bed with Mickey beneath him. Edge savored Mickey's mouth while he reached between them and held their cocks together. He moved against Mickey, making love to him the way he said he would. For his sanity's sake, this was the only sexual interaction they had anymore. He wondered sometimes if he disappointed Mickey, but he couldn't hurt him. Learning he had believed himself straight before now made things worse. Edge wasn't disappointed, though. He just wanted the intimacy.

Mickey strained beneath him, making sounds that had Edge ready to blow. Everything about Mickey made him hot as hell. It suddenly hit him all over again that he had lost this. He had shoved Mickey from his life like it wouldn't fucking kill him.

Edge pressed his forehead against Mickey's and stared into his eyes. "I'm sorry. I'm so fucking sorry." Even he heard the way his voice broke.

Mickey held his face. "Stop. We're fine. Now give me your cum."

Edge never looked away as he tried to do just that. He hadn't known a person could feel so connected to someone else. It got harder to hold his eyes open. The pleasure was too much.

"That's it, beautiful. Come for me."

Edge couldn't disobey. He cried out as cum coated his fingers. Edge didn't stop stroking until Mickey joined him. It was sexy as fuck, watching him blow. His back bowed, and he made a sound that nearly made Edge come again. He had never felt so high on life. Whatever it took, he wouldn't fail Mickey again.

Chapter Nine

DARKNESS ENGULFED THE LIGHT outside
the window. They hadn't left the bedroom. In nothing but their underwear,
they lounged in bed and watched TV. It
was amazing just sitting in silence with
Edge. They toyed with each other's fingers and snuggled. Mickey couldn't get
enough.

The bedroom door flew open, and Ridge
stormed in, looking hard and pissed.
Henry and Beau stood in the doorway
behind him while Ridge grabbed jeans
off the floor and tossed them their way.
"Let's go. They tried to take Shadow."

Edge was up like a flash, hopping into his pants. "Where?"

"Right from the property. They set off the silent alarms and scattered when we burst from the house, but we caught one. He's still alive."

Mickey had no clue what was happening, but he was in. He gathered several people tried to abduct Shadow, and this seemed to be exactly what they stayed prepared for with all their security.

"Fuck. They're getting bold. Is that old fucker still alive?"

Ridge shrugged. "Probably. He knows Rain would come for Shadow."

Mickey didn't even ask questions. Proving why Mickey stayed loyal to Beau, Beau led the way. "Clay, let's go. Fabrice, keep an eye on Kylo."

At his orders, Clay—one of Beau's many guards—shot to his feet and followed. Fabrice pulled a gun from a kitchen drawer and set it on the counter.

"*Oui, Monsieur.*"

Beau headed for the garage. He glanced Ridge's way. "We'll follow. Edge will ride with us."

Ridge nodded and ran for the driveway. They piled into the SUV and Henry gunned it out of the garage. Mickey had so many questions. He wasn't forced to ask.

"I assume your past is still trying to catch you."

At Beau's words, Edge nodded. "They'll never stop. At least not as long as Commander Kuznetsov lives. He's obsessed with Rain. The guy fully believes Rain is his property. That's why we stay to-gether. He knows if he can get to one of us, then he has Rain. Rain would never let any of us get taken, most especially Shadow. That's why Austen moved in with us."

"If he's obsessed and his pride is pricked from Rain slipping through his fingers, then you're right. He won't stop." Beau sounded like a man in the know, because he was that guy. He was powerful and could have whatever he wanted. There was no such thing as escaping him. He would never allow it.

Mickey fucking hated this for so many reasons. Mostly because neither of them could leave their circumstances. What they had now was all they would ever have. The thought made him a lot sad-der than he wanted to admit.

It didn't take them long to reach Edge's place. As always, the door flew open as soon as they reached the front steps. Tracker's closed expression didn't bode well.

Edge pushed past everyone. "Where is the motherfucker? Is Shadow okay?"

"I'm fine." Shadow sat on the couch with Rain. Rain looked pale and shaken. His hands were clasped in his lap and his knuckles were white. Austen tried talking to him, but it was like nothing penetrated. Mickey knew a silent PTSD attack when he saw one. Nothing could have told him more about their pasts than that. Rain and Shadow were the scariest of the bunch. They might be small and delicate-looking, but they were terrifying in the quickness and ease with which they killed. If Rain was affected, this was bad.

"Our visitor is in the garage."

Mickey knew exactly where Tracker meant. It was the same place Edge had taken him after his abduction.

As a unit, they headed that way. It was just one guy. He didn't know why they were all there, especially Beau and Henry. Still, they went together.

The door opened to a horrific sight. If the guy had anything to say, he had definitely talked. Field was covered in blood. His eyes were crazed in a way Mickey had never seen. Tidy and Crisp stood nearby—stone-faced.

"You didn't have to come home."

Edge looked calm, but Mickey felt the tension—like he expected Field might do anything. "I was told the guy was alive."

Field didn't even blink. It was eerie. "He was. Now he isn't. It seems Commander Kuznetsov learned Rain was recently married. He's lost patience. We'll have to take turns guarding Austen. He can't leave this house alone again. Not even to go to the new clinic. It seems even on property, we're no longer safe."

God. Mickey's chest hurt. He couldn't imagine how Rain must feel. No doubt he expected Austen would bolt now. The guy had already given up everything.

"Okay. Get your team together."

Edge didn't question Beau's order, which surprised him a little. "All right, leave this for right now. Field, get cleaned up and meet us in the family room." Edge motioned toward the house. "Everyone else, let's go."

Mickey hung back, letting everyone pass. He would protect their backs. Even though the problem had obviously been resolved, it was his job to always assume a threat could strike at any second.

It took a few minutes for everyone to settle. Beau stood by, watching the entire scene like a patient father. Mickey studied him to give himself a focal point. He had changed so much since Kylo came into their lives. The cold, calculating, and ruthless Beau still existed, but his parental side shined brighter. Everyone in this house was in their twenties. Nearly everyone on Beau's staff had been saved from the streets. Beau had a soft spot he didn't openly show, but he cared. Mickey saw it. After all, Beau had saved him.

Once everyone was gathered, Beau did what he always did. He took control. "You've obviously done an excellent job keeping each other safe over the years. Unfortunately, you have powerful enemies who grow in numbers every day. You'll never be safe without having a just as powerful ally."

It was true. Mickey hoped Beau didn't prick their pride too much. He wasn't done.

"My home is a compound spread across over twelve acres of land nestled in the center of more than fifty acres. Each of the seven buildings are connected by underground tunnels that can also be used as escape routes. Each building also has a minimum of eight bedrooms and eleven bathrooms. It is the most se-cure place in the country, protected by dozens of guards and combat trained staff. The security is top-notch, but I'm sure Tracker can improve anything. I suggest you tour each building and pick a room. If we combine our families, we could be untouchable."

Silence met his words.

Edge looked Mickey's way. They held each other's stare, and a silent mes-sage passed between them. This was the only way they could be together.

Edge cleared his throat. "I'm sure every-one would like a moment to think about it, but I think it's great plan. We won't have to look over our shoulders all the time. Or at least we'd have help to watch our backs. I don't think Commander

Kuznetsov would dare go against the Bosi family. That's way too high of a profile battle. He won't want his organization exposed. Austen would have a much easier time seeing patients." He looked Beau's way. "I'm assuming."

Beau nodded. "There's a suite on the bottom floor of building two that's the perfect location to see patients with high security, and my youngest son's guard now lives with him. His room is empty, which would suit you two nicely. It's very similar to your apartment–style room here... except bigger." He smiled as if hoping they understood he wasn't trying to insult them. Beau focused on Rain. "Plus, Kylo would love to have you there for impromptu dance parties."

Rain took Austen's hand. "You had me at making Austen's life easier. I've never cared where we live."

"I go where Rain goes," Austen said with enough power to leave no doubt their relationship couldn't be broken.

"Me too," Shadow said. "I'm his shadow."

"I go where they go."

At Field's comment, heads nodded. "We're a family. We stay together." Ridge didn't sound thrilled, but it was obvious he would follow the majority.

A bright smile lit Tracker's face. "That's a huge piece of property to secure." He rubbed his hands together. "I love a challenge."

Beau nodded. "It's decided, then. When you're ready, we'll get everyone settled."

The only person who looked angry about the situation was Henry. Not everyone would notice since he always looked stoic, but fury blazed in his eyes. Mickey hated that he felt like they couldn't talk anymore. He wanted to know if it was the extra burden of more people or Mickey that had him looking like he wanted to snap someone's neck. He supposed he would never know. It didn't look like they were friends anymore.

It was probably selfish as hell to uproot his entire family so he could be with Mickey. He wouldn't admit that was the reason he agreed, but he was certain at least a few of his brothers saw right through him. He had never done anything just for himself. Realistically, he knew this was a much better long-term plan for his family than simply hoping they were always quick enough to keep each other safe. Kuznetsov would never give up. Maybe one day he would be dead and possibly they'd be free, but he doubted it. The guy had convinced too many of his comrades that this whole matter was about a loose end that could expose them. It wasn't, of course. The reasons didn't matter. He wanted his family to have as normal of a life as possible. It would never happen without help. They had uprooted their lives twice in the past for Rain and Shadow's career. When would it be his turn? Hopefully, now. That didn't mean he didn't question himself.

"Do you think we're making a mistake? My family, I mean. I jumped on saying yes to Beau, but I'll admit I was only thinking of myself. Plus, still solely thinking of myself here, what if you decide you're done with me? Then I've asked my brothers to join me in this disaster." Edge didn't usually doubt himself or show vulnerability, but it seemed like that was all he had done since falling in love.

Their feet brushed beneath the covers. On their sides, in Mickey's bed, they held each other's stare. It felt intimate. They felt real.

"I guess, if it would make you feel better, you could pick a room as far away from me as possible as a place to go to get away from me. But I'd really love for you to stay right here. As for your family, they really are better off here. I know it'll be an adjustment." Mickey looked unsure for a moment before continuing, as if saying something he shouldn't. "Beau scooped me from the streets when I was seventeen. If he hadn't, I know I'd be dead by now. He's never admitted that he was doing anything more than basically kidnapping me, but I'm not dumb. I've lived here for twenty years. In those years, I've seen a lot of stuff. There's no one Beau loves more than his kids. I think that fatherly affection is bigger than he lets on. He won't stand by and watch your family die." A smile exploded across Mickey's face. "Don't get me wrong, though. You'll be another weapon in his arsenal. He'll use your crew for his own devices, but you'll be under his protection, and I think you'll be happy here." Guilt passed over Mickey's features. "Also, maybe, if your family decides they're miserable here, maybe you could stay anyhow. You'd still be under Beau's protection. You're untouchable here. I hate that I even said that out loud. We're talking about your family. Obviously, you have to always choose them."

Edge's first thought horrified even him. But when he looked at things closer, it was the realest realization he had ever experienced. "I don't know. If push comes to shove, in any situation, I don't think they'd choose me. For once, I want to be picked. I want to be selfish. I want to be with you. Does that make me terrible?"

"It makes you human."

Mickey's immediate answer with zero hesitation lifted a huge weight from Edge's chest. He loved his family, but people grew up and created their own families. Edge felt like that was what was happening with Mickey. Realistically, he knew they hadn't been together that long, but he also knew himself. He didn't feel this way. This wasn't something that happened to him. The only way he felt this strongly and determined was if it was real. Mickey was his one.

"I want to stay right here." A smile exploded across his lips as he sealed the fate he wanted for himself. "To be real, I like my bed better, though. Yours is hard."

"I've got ten years on you. My back hurts. A firmer bed helps." Mickey smiled through every word. He scooted closer. "We can get rid of this and keep yours. The only times my back has ever hurt leaving your bed, it was for different reasons."

God, he made Edge so fucking happy. It was the first time he felt like he could rest. He felt safe. No attack would come tonight.

Mickey kissed the corner of his mouth, making Edge's heart beat faster. "I have a confession. I've been practicing." Confusion crowded Edge's cloudy brain. Thankfully, Mickey didn't stop there. He kissed the other side of Edge's mouth. "So that you won't hurt me."

"Hopefully alone." Edge didn't mean for that to be his reaction, but the confession made him nervous. He never wanted to freak out and risk their relationship again.

Mickey chuckled. It was a low and sexy sound. "Of course. You should know I'm yours." He kept moving closer until he had Edge on his back and straddled Edge's body. They had stripped for bed and nothing stood between him and heaven. Fuck. He would let Mickey have anything, even if it ended badly. Edge couldn't deny him. Plus, Edge genuinely wanted to move past this hump too. He needed them to have the fullest life together possible. Not to mention, Mickey's body was very distracting. The hungry way he kissed always stole all Edge's thoughts.

"Will you trust me?"

Edge barely heard the whispered question between kisses. "Always."

He watched Mickey ready himself. It was a hot show. By the time Mickey slowly lowered himself on Edge's cock, Edge was a panting mess. He kept locking his back teeth in hopes of hiding his over-the-top desperation. The lust won every time. No one could look at Mickey and say he didn't love riding Edge's cock. Edge felt so many things. Mickey worked for them all the time. He fought to keep this relationship moving forward. Edge was the luckiest person alive, and he had no idea how to express that.

"I love you. Fuck, you look so sexy on my dick. I don't deserve you. Swear this is forever. I need to know I'll fall asleep beside you every night for the rest of my life. Please let me be the only person to see you like this." Edge knew he babbled, but he couldn't stop. He was just so addicted to this new experience called happiness. Edge was scared as hell of losing it.

Mickey suddenly went still and nose to nose with Edge. He looked more intense than Edge had ever seen him. "You are mine. Not only will you be in this bed every night from now on, if you touch anyone else, I'll kill them. You're the only man for me. This is it for both of us."

"Okay." While his agreement came out soft and shaky, he had never meant anything more. He had been chosen. Mickey had his love and loyalty for life.

Mickey slowly lowered his head and brushed his lips across Edge's mouth, forcing Edge to chase him. The moment he caught him, their kiss turned heated. It got harder for Edge to focus on anything other than his building pleasure. Sounds came from the back of his throat that matched Mickey's moans. They moved against each other, racing toward the same goal. Mickey cried out and then Edge touched heaven. Every breath stuttered from him as Mickey's body convulsed. Even as he tried breathing through the powerful orgasm, his mind was crystal clear. Never again would he lose this. He would die first.

Chapter Ten

I T HADN'T BEEN A quick process of getting
their entire setup moved from one place
to another. While they hadn't lived in
their house for very many years, they
had chosen to dig in and build a fortress
of sorts. There was more involved than
just moving houses, getting rid of furni-
ture, and figuring out where they would
all stay. The house had to be scrubbed of
all traces of them and Beau's place had
to become Tracker's standard of secure.
But every day, Edge got to be with Mickey
at some point, even if it was only at night
while they relaxed in bed. They always

got at least a couple of hours of quality time before falling asleep.

They were still on the fence about whether they would get rid of the dance studio. There wasn't a good space for them to work at Beau's. While Kylo had a playroom where Shadow and Rain could dance, that was only occasionally, since the room was Kylo's private space. They had been in talks with Beau about breaking ground on a new building to add to his compound. The biggest pain was finding a company they could trust and the security nightmare. Beau had a connection on the east coast who had built homes and warehouses for mafia bosses and other types. He came highly recommended, but they hadn't had a chance to fly the guy out to really get into things. Life had just been in a bit of an upheaval for a few months. Still, Edge couldn't get enough of this new life.

"You're always quiet, but it's different these days. It's like you've found peace."

At Tracker's words, a smile automatically tugged at Edge's lips. It was true. He felt at peace. "I suppose I have. It's almost funny. I spent years sitting quietly and reading, trying to lose myself in books. I thought that was what peace looked like. Strange how it's actually this madness of uprooting everything and scrambling to get everything done while still studying for jobs. Who knew?"

Tracker laughed. "It's Mickey. He's a calm person. I think he's healing you in some way only he can. It's nice. You deserve this. Everyone thinks so. That's really why everyone didn't balk at moving."

Guilt washed over Edge. Tracker drove them to inspect the rooftop of a building of an upcoming job. It was just the two of them, which was rare. Tracker had always joked that Edge was the boss, but Edge had always felt more like Tracker led them. He was the calm one, always in control. Everyone talked to him. If anyone knew the collective thoughts of the group, it was him.

"Damn. I never meant to steal everyone from their home. There's still time for everyone to change their minds. I can go alone. Beau would keep me safe."

Tracker shot him an annoyed look. "We stay together. That was the deal. If we start falling apart, everything goes with it. You know damn well that's when they'll pick us off one by one. They'd know immediately we were down by one man. Maybe they'll even find ways to keep pulling us out one at a time until they have Rain all alone. Setting all that aside, Beau is right. We need a powerful ally. Our plan to dig in never stood a chance of lasting forever. All it would take was enough people and they could overwhelm us. No one would care. No retaliation or repercussions would come. We'd just be dead... if we're lucky."

All that was true. He still felt bad.

Thankfully, Tracker wasn't finished. "With Beau on our side, there're consequences. Kuznetsov won't have government backing. That's too much risk of exposure and losing a powerful connection. They won't chance that happening just for us. Plus, he can't keep saying we're a loose end. We're not now. We've teamed up with one of their biggest weapon suppliers."

"Is Beau supplying weapons to them?" That tidbit was interesting.

Tracker shrugged. "I don't actually know, but it wouldn't surprise me. If not, he's still a possible supplier who's way too big to alienate. Not to mention the blowback they would get if they took out other countries' supplier. It's not just us anymore. We have friends. Plus, it's not like we have to sit at breakfast with the guy. We have our own space. A pretty fucking nice space, I might add." Tracker suddenly looked excited. "When I talked to Beau this morning, he said he heard back from that guy on the east coast. His name is Bryson, and he's pumped to help us expand. Beau wants him to build us a garage on our side of the property, so we have plenty of space for our vehicles, and he's building me a special security space that'll be decked out with everything, and I mean everything. It'll be so cool to have my own domain."

The happiness in Tracker's voice warmed Edge's chest. He truly hoped everyone had the same level of excitement about moving. They wouldn't be all in the same space any longer. With their choice of rooms all over the place, Edge imagined the guys would just choose one that fit them. Edge, of course, would be in the main house with Mickey. Mickey couldn't go far from Kylo. He needed to be within shouting distance. There were still several extremely nice rooms that sat empty in the main house, but Edge doubted they would

choose those. He couldn't imagine anyone wanted to sit at breakfast with
Beau, as Tracker had said. Austen and
Rain had already moved all their things
into an extremely nice suite, while a few
others still weren't settled. Since Austen
was friends with the Bosi family, he
didn't mind taking the guard's bedroom
Beau had suggested in the main house.
To Edge's surprise, Field had taken the
bedroom next to him and Mickey, even
though it was small. He said he didn't
want to be far from Mickey. While that
might be partially true, Edge knew him.
A small room was probably his way
of accepting less since he couldn't give
Beau anything in exchange for the place
to live. Edge had a bad feeling that was
wrecking his mental health a little. He
had been off since the move. Shadow
and Ridge had also chosen rooms near-

by. The rest would likely stick to wherever their usual clique went. He supposed time would tell.

Tracker put the van in park, making Edge realize he had been lost in thought. The poor guy probably thought Edge didn't care about all the news he had just been excited to share. He threw as much happiness into his voice as he could. "That's really amazing about you getting your own space. Obviously, Beau sees your worth. You deserve that." He realized it was true. If they had been allowed to go their own ways, this was exactly what Edge pictured for Tracker—him flexing his skills in a career with a powerful client.

"Thanks, man. Just think. If you hadn't kidnapped Mickey, we might not have gotten here. We'd still be looking over our shoulders for the rest of our lives."

He appreciated Tracker making him feel better about thinking about himself for once. "That's what I've always wanted for us."

Tracker flashed him a smile before climbing from the van. Edge grabbed his gear and followed. Tracker pointed toward the building. "You go ahead to the roof, and I'll head inside and take the stairs. That way, I can check on possible positions for various cameras."

With a nod, Edge didn't hesitate to hit the alley. He studied the wall for a second before picking a spot and heading up. It was much easier than the schematics had made it look. When he reached the top, he almost fell. Shock tried rendering his arms useless. His entire family waited on the roof. They were all smiles. It took him a second to realize Mickey was at the front of the crowd... on one knee.

Edge shuffled closer. His entire body was numb, and he had no idea how his feet managed to work. But in a matter of moments, he stared down at an open ring box and a smiling but nervous-looking Mickey.

He didn't waste words. "Will you marry me?"

Edge blinked. His vision darkened around the edges. He swayed.

Mickey shot to his feet and hauled Edge against him to keep him steady. "Whoa. Are you okay?"

"Yes, and yes."

Mickey pulled away a hair to meet his gaze. "Was that a yes to my proposal?"

Edge nodded. It felt like wildest of head bobs. "Yes. Fuck yeah." His voice gained in strength. "I just can't believe you want to keep me."

"Here. Take this ring." Mickey shoved the ring box into Edge's hands, leaving him free to squeeze Edge until he could barely breathe. "You're mine. Of course I want to keep you. Now breathe before you pass out."

Everyone smiled and clapped, congratulating them. He watched Tracker pop open a bottle of champagne, and everything felt so surreal. Edge didn't even know how Tracker had gotten there so quickly. His entire brain was just a fog of disbelief.

Edge's throat swelled. He tried to take a proper breath, but it still didn't happen. At Mickey's concerned look, Edge broke. "You don't understand. I'll have a genuine family. You'll be my family. I can't believe you'd do that for me."

"Why are you talking like I'm doing you some kind of favor? I love you."

Edge couldn't let go of him long enough to even look at the ring. The shock slowly lifted. A laugh burst from him. "I can't believe you put this together. Did we even get a job offer or was this whole thing a setup?"

Rain appeared with two glasses of champagne. "It was a setup. You have no idea how hard you are to surprise."

Field raced to their other side and hauled them into his huge embrace. "I'm so happy for you two. We get to keep Mickey!"

The truth sank in a little more by the second. This was really happening. He couldn't believe it. Mickey wanted to be legally tied to him forever. Holy shit. His smile grew. Edge finally took the ring from the box and put it on. It was a little loose, but he was too fucking ecstatic to care.

"I love it." Edge really did, even though his brain still refused to cling to any details. Then his chin lifted, and he stared into the green eyes that had stolen him the very first time he saw them. "I love you."

A champagne glass pressed into his hand. Still, Edge didn't look away. Even as toasts were made and the guys made plans like they were about to have a wedding that day. All Edge saw was the face of the man he loved. The man who had pulled him away from the edge of madness. For the first time in his life, the only emotion that existed for him was love.

Keep an eye out for the next Killers Inc., *Deranged.*

About the Author

CHARITY PARKERSON IS AN award-winning and multi-published author with several companies. Born with no filter from her brain to her mouth, she decided to take this odd quirk and insert it in her characters. One of her greatest loves is writing morally gray characters. You'll find them scattered throughout her hundreds of titles.

*Nine-time Readers' Favorite Award Winner

*2015 Passionate Plume Award Finalist

*2013 Reviewers' Choice Award Winner

*2012 ARRA Finalist for Favorite Para-
normal Romance

*Five-time winner of The Mistress of
the Darkpath

Connect with her online:

*Sign up for her newsletter: https://bi
t.ly/charityparkersonnewsletter

*Join her readers' group on Facebook:
http://bit.ly/CharitysTribe

*Website: https://www.charityparker
son.com

*A list of her social media accounts and
giveaways all in one place: http://hy.pa
ge/charityparkerson